THE SPRING

THE SPRING

MEGAN WEILER

JACKLEG PRESS

JackLeg Press
www.jacklegpress.org

ISBN: 978-1-7373307-9-0

Library of Congress Control Number: 2021948322

Cover design by Richard Every.
Cover photo by William Caferro.

The Spring is a work of fiction. Any resemblance to people, either
alive or dead, or actual events is coincidental.

For Bill

"You learn to know a country that is fundamentally quite different from its appearance at first sight."

Vincent Van Gogh,
Letter to Theo

I: *SUMMER 1996*

1

As I am putting away my groceries I find a dead mouse next to the refrigerator. I bend over to look more closely. It is surrounded by a sort of halo, lying in a bed of soft mold which in turn has dried out long ago. The house has been empty for over a year. I put on rubber gloves to pick the mouse up and throw it down the hill. The little carcass feels stiff and shockingly light. It is so light that it does not fly very far.

Since my stomach is already queasy, I decide to tackle the small bathroom upstairs right away. I try the faucets in the sink, although I know nothing will come out. The wooden shutter must have blown open at some point—the latch is loose—and the entire room is black with bat droppings. Fortunately the door was shut, otherwise the whole house would be covered. Bat droppings are not much different from mouse droppings, small and dry, with only a faint smell. Still I repeatedly gag as I sweep the floor, and have to run outside for fresh air. I clean the sink and toilet with generous amounts of Windex, throw away the soap and the soap dish for good measure.

The rest of the house is as might be expected after being empty for so long. Spiders' webs everywhere, dust and crumbling plaster. I go from room to room opening windows and shutters, letting the warm May air flow in until doors start slamming from the cross-draft. The violent sounds feel like blows, driving home what I already know. The cisterns are empty. I have no water at all.

For all my doubts about coming to Querceto, my family's house in Tuscany, it never occurred to me that water could be a problem. It's only May, too early for the spring to have dried up.

It was a long trip from America, where I live now. I arrived in Florence and spent the night in a dingy hotel near the train station. This morning, just a few hours ago, I was still happily ignorant, unsuspecting. I woke up early and strolled through the empty streets.

Looking back, though, I feel that I had a kind of premonition on the last part of my journey, like a blindfolded person being led by the hand, gently but firmly, right up to this disaster that was waiting for me.

On the train to Vigliano I began to feel apprehensive. Usually I love looking out the windows at the wheat and corn fields and shimmering olive groves; at the old villas and farmhouses set back into the hills and the newer buildings near the train tracks, with their kitchen gardens and laundry strung out on balconies. But this time, I gazed out without really seeing anything, wrapped in a vague anxiety.

When I arrived in Vigliano I went to retrieve our Fiat Uno from the woman at the car wash, who charges astronomical sums to shelter it in her garage, then uses it secretly for taxi runs on the worst country tracks, sparing her own minivan. She flashed a big sharp-toothed smile at me, as if overjoyed to see me again after all this time, and I didn't have the courage to argue over the bill. Because of this, I had too little money left for buying groceries. I miscalculated and had to return some items, annoying the people behind me in line.

Driving up the long steep hill past the tiny village of Cetinale, on the unpaved road slippery with loose dirt and stones, the Uno continually threatened to stall. I turned the hairpin curve at the farm called Riaccio and five or six big sheep dogs came running out, barking ferociously and racing alongside the car, so close that they seemed to disappear under the wheels. I couldn't slow down because if I lost momentum I wouldn't make it to the top. Those dogs always terrify me, no matter how much I tell myself they are only playing. When I had finally outstripped them and reached even ground at the cluster of houses known as La Croce, my heart was pounding.

After La Croce the road dwindles to a bumpy path. The car rolled easily down the last small slope. I felt a pang of joy at the sight of Querceto. The house looked overgrown, but it was still the same, still *there*, in its simple rectangular shape and worn fieldstone.

The key fit in the lock, and it turned. Tugging open the wooden outer door past the thick wad of grass that had grown in front of it, I noticed irises by the side of the house. But now was not the time to stop and admire them. A sense of foreboding pressed me on. There was a sound of tearing cobwebs as I opened the inner door. I picked up the flashlight at the bottom of the stairs, but the batteries were dead, so I groped my way up to the fuse box in the bedroom. I flicked the heavy switch. Lights went on. I ran back down to the kitchen and found the instructions for activating the water pump taped to the wall. I followed them carefully, attaching the electrical cord before going to the *stallina*, the outbuilding which houses the cisterns.

I heard the motor start up. So the pump had not burst in the winter. With each little success, my panic grew.

And here it was. Lifting the broken lid, I stared

down into the cistern, from which a musty smell rose up. I couldn't see all the way to the bottom, but I knew that it was empty; I could feel it. As if to show me, a centipede climbed over the edge and disappeared into the dark.

Now that I knew the worst, I felt almost calm.

I have bottled water enough to last me a couple of days. I must think about what I am going to do.

I finish unloading the car, carry my suitcase and my satchel filled with books and notebooks upstairs. Sealed up in one of the steamer trunks I find clean sheets, pillows, and a blanket smelling of mothballs. I make up the bed in the largest bedroom, with its sloping roof beams that are like the ribbing of an enormous wing.

As a child, I had mixed feelings about this place. We used to come several times a year, driving down from Germany. I didn't share my parents' enthusiasm for working on the house, for stripping wood and painting and digging drainage ditches. I sometimes wished that we could have spent our vacations on a beach or in the mountains like other people.

But now an emotion fills me as I move through

the rooms—like coming home. Or rather, it's as though I'd never left; as if, throughout all the changes in my life, in some part of my brain I have always been here.

I go back down to the kitchen and make strong coffee using bottled water. I heat milk on the gas burner, frothing it with a whisk. I cut slices of bread from the big loaf I've bought and spread them with jam. I eat my meal outside on the terrace, a rectangle of lichen-covered stones facing west. In the stillness, I hear a mockingbird and a woodpecker on the hill above the house, and then a human cry somewhere in the distance below. Probably Renato shouting to his son Lorenzo, as they work together on a field.

The idea of coming to Querceto occurred to me one evening after my brother and I had once again talked on the phone about selling the place. We have both moved to America. The distance is now too great, and we don't have the means to keep the house up. But it's a decision neither of us wants to face.

I had been going through a difficult time, and I thought that a change of scene might help me. I had some money saved up; I could request a leave from my job. My idea was to take advantage of the peace and solitude to finish my dissertation, which I abandoned when I left university. A degree serves no purpose in my life now, but the unfinished thesis has been at the back of my mind, giving me a feeling of dissatisfaction with myself.

I called my brother back and told him of my plan. There was a silence at the other end of the line. "All alone?" he finally said. "Are you sure?"

It seemed to me that he was pleased, and perhaps a little envious.

Ants have begun to mobilize, struggling to carry away the crumbs I drop. A bumble bee motors along. Two lizards chase each other across the terrace stones and disappear into the weeds.

This humming, peaceful activity carries on day after day. It hasn't stopped since the last time I sat here; it will continue after I leave. When my family first came to Querceto, Lorenzo was a toddler and it was Renato's father, Bruno, who shouted across the field. Now Lorenzo is grown; soon there will be another generation. But the buzzing, the warbling, and the peculiar acoustics which make faraway sounds seem close at hand—these things will always be the same.

In all of it there is a great indifference toward me, a cosmic not-caring whether I stay or leave. Without water, I'll have to leave. A feeling of despair comes over me at the thought of having to go down to Florence and book a flight back to America.

2

When my family first came to the Mugello region in the early seventies, it seemed a corner of the world forgotten by time. The town of Vigliano is only an hour away from Florence by train, on the route leading north to Borgo San Lorenzo. But back then, the peasants still plowed their fields with white oxen. There were few foreigners, and we were greeted with friendly curiosity and hospitality offered in poor but impeccably clean kitchens. The peasants were living a near-extinct way of life as sharecroppers under the medieval system of *mezzadria*, owing half their yield to the landowner. Many of them were leaving the land. Their houses stood empty, deserted.

The Fattoria Poggiogriffini, comprising a stately villa and a dozen peasant farmhouses scattered in the hills above it, was owned by a man whom everyone simply called *il Marchese*. In his youth he had been a prize-winning equestrian, a member of Mussolini's elite cavalry. He got his title, we were told, by marrying the daughter of Italy's ambassador to Berlin. After the war he had lived for a long time in South America. When he finally returned to Italy, his son-in-law, an oil man from Texas, bought him this estate for his retirement.

Now in his sixties, the Marchese still had a trim figure and a proud military bearing. He knew nothing about agriculture. The only thing he cared about was horses. He was secretly relieved when the peasants, destitute, began to leave. He sold off their houses, each with its own beautiful name, for practically nothing, amazed that anyone would want to pay money for crumbling piles of stone. He asked his realtor to give preference to German buyers, because when all was said and done, he still felt most comfortable among Germans.

Querceto was one of these houses, perched high on the side of a hill. It was in bad shape—the roof leaked in fifteen places and the upstairs floors were caving in. The last person to have lived on the ground floor was a shepherd, who had left his racks for drying cheese in the kitchen. Two other rooms had served as a *stalla*, a barn for cows; they had troughs and were filled with manure. But the basic structure was sound. The rooms were high and spacious and cool even in the summer, with their thick stone walls. And when you stepped out the back door you could see the entire valley spread out below, a wide, unobstructed view all the way to the blue mountains in the distance.

There were two side buildings: the *stallina*, with

10

cubicles for fowl and rabbits, and a half-ruined structure we called the bake house, because it had a wood oven for baking bread in front.

Water was a problem from the beginning. The first night that we came to stay in the house, the faucets were dry. The four of us, my parents, my brother, and I, walked over to the cluster of houses on the next hill, each carrying a pot or a pitcher, whatever we could find. There, at La Croce, we met the Donati family—Costanzo and Silvana and their teenaged son Enrico. We sat in their tiny kitchen, making some sort of conversation with our few words of Italian. Costanzo and Silvana were the same age as my parents, but they looked much older. And there was that other strange boy, Flavio, who didn't come into the kitchen but peeked around the edge of the door frame and stared at us through the window, scampering back and forth while making the sounds of a dog or a cat.

Costanzo and Silvana said, "Come and visit us again tomorrow." In the years that followed they repeated this invitation often, earnestly. They'd say: "Come over, *per compagnia*, because together is better than alone."

How quiet the night was all around as we carefully carried our filled vessels back on the rutted path, walking in silence like some strange religious procession. The earth was like black velvet and the sky was filled with stars.

After that we got used to carrying water in buckets up the steep hill on the other side of Querceto, from a tap outside a house called Casabassa, which was then still inhabited, though not for long, by Mario, his wife Franca, and their son Marcello, who later became a butcher, a *macellaio*, as if taking his cue from his own name.

One of the first steps my parents took to make Querceto habitable was to have two small connecting cisterns, each holding five hundred liters, installed in the *stallina*. The cisterns were fed through a black rubber tube from a spring higher up in the hills, a few kilometers away. It was written into the contract that Querceto shared the rights to the spring with Casabassa and another house, Pruneto, on whose property it was located. The hills were veined with these rubber tubes, an inch or so in diameter, that ran alongside the paths, half-buried in the earth or hidden by brambles, carrying precious trickles of water over long distances. A small electric pump pushed the water from the cisterns up into the house. I remember our excitement the first time this system actually worked and water came out of the faucet in the kitchen.

What we didn't realize was that the problem of water would only become more complicated and elusive. When the cisterns were empty, there were now any number of possible causes.

The Mugello has changed over the years. Like the rest of Tuscany, it gradually became overrun with foreigners, jostling each other in the little local supermarkets while still pretending to themselves that they were pioneers. Those who have been here longer look down upon the relative newcomers, who are generally richer and had to pay more money for less desirable houses.

When *mezzadria* was legally abolished, there was one peasant left on the estate who was able to buy his farm. Renato Montanari, Silvana's nephew, is intelligent and hard-working. He has grown more prosperous each year, buying up fields left and right. Instead of the oxen that his father used, Renato has John Deere tractors standing by the side of his house. Instead of seven cows he has forty, housed in a fully automated barn bought at the agricultural fair in Verona.

The Marchese tried unsuccessfully to breed first horses and then goats on his remaining land, and squandered all the money that came to him from the sale of the houses. Finally he had to sell the Villa itself.

He retired with his wife, *la Marchesa,* a tiny woman frail as a twig, to a cottage down the road.

The Villa has since been resold several times, undergoing renovations under each of its owners, none of whom ever came to live in it.

Querceto has stayed as it was first built, a simple block, unlike many other farmhouses which acquired complicated shapes as they were enlarged for growing families. On entering, the first thing you see is the stone staircase leading up to the second floor. To the right is the room that was once the kitchen, with a hooded fireplace—big enough to accommodate three people sitting on either side of the fire—and a stone sink from the days before running water. Though we call it the living room, it is rarely used; you go through it into what is now the kitchen, the most important place in the house. This large room is pleasant and inviting, especially in summer, when the double doors are kept open to the terrace and the valley. It has an uneven terracotta tile floor, in the center of which stands our dining table: a heavy antique library table made of oak, with baroque angels carved into the legs. The rest of the furniture is a miscellany of rustic pieces. There is a wood stove in the corner, but the cooking is done on a three-ring gas burner. A long high shelf, formerly the side of a trough, bears pots and pans and odds and ends, including decades-old dried herbs. Most of life at Querceto is spent between the kitchen and the terrace, which has become the true front of the house. Now, when visitors come, they go straight to the back.

From the kitchen you enter the *stalla*, the left half of the house. Only semi-restored, it serves as a repository for tools and supplies; the troughs contain stacks of tiles and kindling. Upstairs are four bedrooms, two large ones above the *stalla* and two smaller ones on the right side, plus the bathrooms, the *gabinetto* or toilet and the *bagno*, which has a little sitting tub and a gas water heater above it.

I roam through the house, making it mine. I love running up and down the stairs. The bedroom I've chosen is the large one in front, facing east and south. It has an iron bedstead, a nightstand, a wardrobe, a chest of drawers, and a desk—a table topped with an old door—where I intend to do my reading and writing, looking out the window toward the bake house and La Croce. I've put my bags in another bedroom; that will be my messy room.

Overcome with exhaustion and jetlag, I lie down on the bed.

I wake up with a start. The phone is ringing downstairs. I reach for my watch on the nightstand and see that it's three o'clock. I've been asleep for two hours.

"There you are! How *wonderful!*" It's Libby, calling from Castellina, a house farther up in the hills. I smile happily at the distinctive sound of her British accent. I suddenly feel less alone.

"We saw the shutters open on our way back from the Co-op. We hoped it might be you. How long has it been?"

The Parkers came to the Mugello at the same time as my family, but they live here year-round. When I was a teenager, Libby found me a summer job in Florence. We've been friends ever since. She doesn't wait for me to answer her question.

"How long are you staying? You've got to come up and see the progress we've made on the house. Can you come tomorrow for tea? Richard got a whole package of *bomboloni*: you can help us eat them. The studio is almost finished!"

I tell her I have no water.

"Ask Renato. He'll know what's up, don't worry. It'll all be sorted out."

Talking to Libby reassures me. She is the kind

16

of person who gives the impression that no difficulty is insurmountable if you just forge ahead and confront it straight-on.

3

In the evening after eight I go to pay a visit to Costanzo and Silvana. It is not yet dark outside. The path leading to La Croce is lined with Scotch broom bushes, whose yellow flowers fill the air with a heavy, sweet fragrance.

The door to their house usually stands slightly ajar. I call *"Permesso?"* through the curtain of plastic strands. There is a brief silence during which I imagine them exchanging glances; then I hear Silvana say something in a low voice.

Silvana comes to the door. "Oh, Cristina, it's you! When did you arrive?" She laughs and hugs me. Without moving from the kitchen, Costanzo calls out: "Cristina! Come in, come in!"

Theirs is the central and smallest house in the cluster called La Croce. In addition there are two larger houses, a small school building, a tiny chapel, and several sheds constructed out of corrugated metal and old highway billboards.

La Croce was never part of the Marchese's estate; it used to be an independent farm. But neither Costanzo nor his cousin Elio has been able to subsist on farming. Both of them work on the national highway grass-cutting crews.

The narrow hallway leading from the Donatis' front door seems built on a scale for the smaller people of a past era. On entering the kitchen, so tiny it cannot easily accommodate more than two visitors at once, I see that they are in the midst of eating what appear to be noodles and pieces of beef in broth. I glance up at the red plastic clock above the table. It's the normal visiting time.

"I hope I'm not disturbing..."

The square window above the sink, cut into a wall two feet deep, is like the porthole of a ship's cabin.

"No, no, come on, sit down." Costanzo, who is not as far progressed with his meal as Silvana, pushes his plate away, saying that he isn't hungry anyway. Silvana explains that they are eating late because they've been down to Florence.

"Sit down, sit down."

We go through the familiar ritual in which I refuse the chair Silvana offers me and instead insist on sitting in my usual spot inside the fireplace. The little bench on one side of it has been my place since I was a child, the smallest person in the group.

"Come on, take this chair, you'll be more comfortable!"

Costanzo waves her off, smiling: "Leave her

19

alone. She always sits there, always. It's her place."

He is a sturdy, muscular man, not very tall, whose eyes seem to be perpetually squinting into the sun. His thick hair is a mixture of straw-colored and gray. While Silvana clears the table, he pulls his chair a few feet back to his usual place, by the gas cooking stove to my right.

Since that first evening when we went to ask for water, I have sat in the Donatis' kitchen countless times. In those early days, more people lived at La Croce: the painter Amedeo, his sister Marietta the schoolteacher, her Sardinian husband Salvatore, and others whom we could never remember or keep apart. Sometimes there would be large gatherings on summer nights, the voices and Amedeo's accordion music carrying over to Querceto.

Now La Croce is quiet in the evenings. Amedeo has died, and Marietta and Salvatore spend half the year in Sardinia. The huge house below Costanzo and Silvana's contains only Elio, his wife Paola, and their son Flavio, who slip in and out like ghosts. The house at the top of the cluster, closest to Querceto, belongs to Florentines who come for the weekend, and the school building, at the farthest end, has been converted into a summer home by a German couple known by their Italianized names as Maia and Manfredo. They have installed a picture window facing the direction of Riaccio.

Perhaps I want to appear as unchanged to Costanzo and Silvana as they appear to me. Unconsciously I imagine that if I make myself small enough to fit into my old spot, they will still see me as a twelve-year-old. It's not until I am sitting on the bench in a slightly hunched, uncomfortable position, one leg crossed over the other so as to take up the least amount of space, that I begin to feel at ease.

"So you're still living down there in America?"

Silvana poses the question with a dreamy smile as if asking to be told a familiar tale one more time. She refers to the whole rest of the world as *laggiù*, "down there." Before, it was "down there in Germany." This is because from La Croce, as from Querceto, you have a clear view of the horizon in all directions but one. The earth's curvature is evident. Any place not visible is obviously lower.

She sits facing me, a tiny person with sharp features softened by the sweetness of her expression, always on the lookout for a reason to smile or laugh. She is dressed in various layers that add up to a complicated ensemble of faded floral fabrics and knits, topped off with an old cardigan. She sits with her arms crossed over her stomach, hugging herself as if she were cold.

"How many hours does it take by plane to get here from America?"

It used to be, "How many hours to drive here from Germany?"

How many kilometers, how high do planes fly; what is the price of gasoline down there, in Germany? For years, when we visited the Donatis, our conversations, hampered by our poor knowledge of Italian, consisted of nothing but this.

When I ask about them, Silvana answers with a pregnant "So-so…" It turns out their trip to Florence was to see a medical specialist about Costanzo, who has been suffering from mysterious ailments. "My head was spinning." He has even stopped going to work for the past two months. No one can say what is wrong with him. They gave him all kinds of tests and, finally, a CT scan.

"That is the last test they give a person." Silvana's grave tone suggests the medical equivalent of last rites. "With that, they see everything, everything." But they didn't see anything. The doctor finally diagnosed Costanzo as having "general depression."

"My right ear was stopped up, too."

"Ssh—that had nothing to do with it, that was something different."

"No, but still," Costanzo insists, shaking his head. "I had all these different disturbances."

As he says it, I notice a swelling on his cheek, probably a large pimple.

"In the beginning, Silvana had to give me injections."

"In his buttocks," she adds, giggling.

Now he is down to two pills a day, one in the morning, one at night. They seem to be helping.

I refrain from pressing them with medical questions, remembering what they said when Silvana's brother Mario became mute: "The vein in his head from which speech comes out is stopped up." Silvana thinks Costanzo's problem is "a kind of change of life, like women have." I suggest exhaustion, from working too much.

"Only seven more months before I retire," Costanzo says. "Then, if I feel like getting up at six, I'll get up at six; if I feel like getting up at eight, I'll get up at eight."

He makes this statement with a stubborn expression, looking down at the floor as if to say, "I don't care what anyone thinks."

Silvana laughs a little and looks at him doubtfully from the side.

I feel great affection for these two people, who

have known each other since they were children. Costanzo has always lived at La Croce, while Silvana grew up at Casabassa. Now she sits there pulling her cardigan tighter, wondering what is going on inside her husband.

"And what about you?"

I tell them that I've broken up with my boyfriend, who was with me the last time I was here. They look startled, but I say it with a shrug and a smile so that they won't question me further. The Italian word for boyfriend is *fidanzato*. That makes it sound worse.

I never know what to say about myself. It's easier to talk about things in the Mugello; this is our common ground. Silvana tells me that Alvise, their grandson, is learning to play soccer in school. Enrico, their son, is only a few years older than me.

"You'll see him soon!"

Costanzo asks how long I am planning to stay.

"I don't know exactly. As long as possible. But I have a big problem: there's no water at Querceto. Do you have any idea why this could be?"

Their reaction is curious. Their faces seem to cloud over. I have the impression they've been steeling themselves for the moment when I would bring this up.

"Oh yes," Costanzo says knowingly. "Everybody has a water shortage. It hasn't been raining. It's a problem for everyone."

Silvana nods, but looks away into a corner.

"But it's not that I have little. I have none at all. There isn't even a drop in the cisterns. There must be some other reason." I grow a little agitated. "I can't stay here without water."

I catch a glance that passes between them.

Costanzo says: "It must be the Cavinis." He is referring to the people who own Pruneto, Florentines who come on the weekends. The spring on which Querceto and Casabassa depend is located on their property.

"They always use a lot. You'll see, tomorrow they'll leave, and then you'll have water again."

It occurs to me that by introducing an explanation different from the one he gave at first, he is canceling out the credibility of both. Besides, this new explanation makes even less sense in light of the fact that there is nothing at all in the cisterns.

But my impression that he is not being quite truthful comes most strongly from the fact that instead of sharing my concern, he seems to be dismissing it. Silvana, though she says nothing, has the uneasy look of honest people when they are forced to lie.

Before leaving, I give myself a push and produce the gift I've brought for them, a small crystal bowl. My reasoning in buying it was that things made of crystal seem to be prized, though I can see nothing attractive about it. But now, as I hand Silvana the parcel with mumbled phrases, I am again unsure. They thank me with an embarrassed air, and Silvana whisks the bowl and its wrapping out of the room as if to remove all traces of a gaffe I had made.

Costanzo says: "If you need anything, like the grass cut around the house or vegetables from the garden, just let us know."

4

In the morning I've decided on my first step. I will call
Giuliano Landi, the *idraulico*, who will sell me water.
He can bring several hundred liters of it with his
tractor. That will buy me time. Landi is Renato's friend,
or perhaps a relative. He lives close by. Often my
parents, finding the pump broken on our arrival
because water had frozen in it during the winter, called
Landi to bring a new one. There are still two or three
defunct pumps lying in the *stallina* next to the most
recent one that works.

But it's not easy to reach Landi. Each time I call,
I get a different family member on the phone, telling
me he isn't home. I try to picture them from their
voices: his wife, brusque, energetic, calling me *Signora*;
his sullen son. An older woman, probably his mother,
is monosyllabic at first, distrustful; then suddenly she
bursts out in heavy dialect: "No way he'll be home
before three!" I get Landi's wife on the phone again
and explain the problem to her. She says she will tell
him to bring me water first thing tomorrow.

I am taking an exploratory walk around the house

when I notice a human figure down at Casabassa. The Wenzels are here, I think. It takes a few moments before my brain processes some further information. The human figure, Johannes Wenzel, is holding a green watering hose.

It can't be: yes, it's true. My mind starts working feverishly. This isn't right. If Querceto doesn't have water, they shouldn't have water either. We share the same spring, the same tube. The water comes through the tube first to Querceto, then to Casabassa. This is because Querceto is higher: if it went to Casabassa first, Querceto would have none at all.

I vaguely remember that there used to be a little cement box sunk into the ground somewhere near the *stallina*. It had a lid you could lift off, and inside was the branching-off of the water tube for Querceto's cisterns on the one hand and Casabassa on the other. By closing a valve, the water could be prevented from flowing down to Casabassa. When Wenzel first bought Casabassa, a latecomer to the Mugello, my father made what he considered to be a joke, saying, "You know we can turn the water off on you." Wenzel, a cardiologist from Stuttgart, did not find this funny.

Of course my father would never have thought of doing this. We scarcely ever opened the cement box, and now the grass is so high that I wouldn't know where to look for it. But ever since that unfortunate "joke," our relationship with the Wenzels, our closest neighbors, has been minimal, limited to curt greetings in passing.

There was another incident that added to the reciprocal coolness. The year after the Wenzels' arrival, their five blond children, joined by two boys from another German family, roamed the countryside as a small gang, exploring empty houses. Silvana said afterwards that she heard a loud banging at Querceto and was surprised because she didn't know there would be builders at work. By the time she got there, they had broken in the door and penetrated as far as the kitchen. They fled down the hill when they saw her, taking with them a pair of scissors and an ax. The parents, when confronted, claimed that their children had found these items in the woods.

In any case we always felt a little contemptuous of the Wenzels, who were down at the bottom of the hill, "in the gulch," as my father used to say, where there was no view at all and Renato's cows brought with them a constant plague of flies. Renato owns a little shed across from the Wenzels' house, along with some sort of partial right to the water; he keeps two or three cows there at all times. Does he do it with the express purpose of irking the *tedesco*, this German who shows up in a Mercedes van so large it is really a small bus? Our sympathies have tended to be with Renato.

But now it's necessary to put old prejudices aside. I must speak to Wenzel. Perhaps he has somehow managed to reverse the situation, so that he can now turn the water off on us. As unlikely as this is, it suddenly seems very foolish not to have cultivated better relations with our neighbor over the years.

It's been so long since I've seen Wenzel up close that I hardly recognize him. He is tall and thin with a narrow head, light brown hair. He looks surprisingly youthful. He seems to watch my approach down the hill skeptically at first, as if uncertain how to act. Then he makes up his mind and comes toward me in long strides, extending his right hand for a hearty shake.

"Welcome! We haven't seen each other in a long time!"

With my peripheral vision I see a shadow flit into the house—probably Frau Wenzel.

The story I've heard is that Johannes Wenzel bought Casabassa sight unseen. Having been shown pictures of a colleague's house in the Mugello and being too busy to come down and look for one himself, he asked his colleague to buy a house for him. His wife hated Casabassa from the moment she set eyes on it, and now Wenzel and his colleague are no longer on speaking terms.

Wenzel offers me a wicker chair on the graveled terrace he's made in front of the house. In Mario's day, the dirt road used to pass right by the front door, the way it does at most farmhouses. The Wenzels had it moved twenty meters away and surrounded their property with a high chain-link fence. They've even planted hedges for privacy.

"Can I offer you some of Renato's wine? He makes his own, you know. We always get it from him. It's not bad."

Wenzel seems happy to have company, even if it's just me. Perhaps he feels isolated and friendless in his Tuscan farmhouse.

I decide to come right to the point.

"I have a big problem," I tell him. "I just arrived yesterday, and I was planning to stay for a while, but I have no water at all. Nothing. Then I saw you watering your garden."

Wenzel doesn't answer me right away. A little smile has appeared on his face. He sits there looking at me as if he were enjoying this moment and wanted to prolong it. I feel my ears grow warm.

"I will tell you a secret now," he says finally. He leans forward confidentially. "The reason we have water right now is that Landi sold us two thousand liters. You know Landi? Do you know what two thousand liters of water cost us? And he gets it for free from the municipal water line in Vigliano. That is of course a ridiculous situation. Ridiculous! But what is one to do? We feel completely helpless!"

He leans back again and seems, despite his words, very pleased. At any rate he is still smiling.

"I've already called Landi myself," I say, crestfallen. "He's coming tomorrow morning. But of course that's not a solution."

"Of course not! Of course it isn't! But our time here is limited. I have to be back in the hospital the day after tomorrow. Perhaps *you* are in a better position to do something. You speak Italian, don't you? I keep taking my evening classes, but to be honest, the results leave much to be desired."

He goes inside to get the wine and returns accompanied by Frau Wenzel, who seems less than enthusiastic about meeting me. I imagine she was dragged out against her will. She is a heavy-set woman with small features sandwiched between plump cheeks.

"*Fräulein* Christine has come by to discuss the

water situation," Wenzel announces importantly, by way of introduction. "We want to join forces and come up with some kind of strategy."

His wife throws him a jaundiced look. "Do you also not have water?" she asks, addressing me.

Wenzel smiles apologetically. "My wife didn't want to come here at all this summer, after her accident last year."

I look questioningly from one to the other. Frau Wenzel peevishly raises the hem of her long, tent-like dress to show me her ankle, which is crisscrossed with scars.

"My foot will never be the same."

She'd been putting up lace curtains in the bedroom, and fell off the stool. It was a complicated and painful fracture. They drove to the hospital at Careggi, more than an hour away, where she was so frightened by the alien surroundings that she pleaded in tears to be brought back to Stuttgart, even though her leg was swelling dangerously.

"And then to drive through the night," Wenzel says slowly, "with your wife screaming at the top of her lungs the whole way..." He looks at me as if asking me to imagine it.

The accident only confirmed the ill omen that had hovered about the house from the start.

"When I bought it," Wenzel says, "my father-in-law said that it was the worst investment I would ever make." And so far this has proven true. It's a drain on their finances. First the road had to be moved; then the structural problems started appearing one by one. Just when they thought it was all done and they could put the curtains up, the ceilings began to cave in.

All of this sounds very familiar to me.

"One room is already completely unusable," Frau Wenzel laments. "And the window shutters need to be done all over again. Even a doctor's salary is not enough, especially when you have five children. And now on top of everything, the water problem."

"Everything is against us. But you know," Wenzel leans forward again, "you know, I think to myself, you just have to dig in. You have to fight for every inch of ground. You have to sink your claws into the earth and not let go."

He asks me whether I've seen a certain article that appeared in the *Frankfurter Allgemeine*, about why people buy Tuscan farmhouses. I haven't.

"Then I won't give it away. It was very well written, very well written. Witty, but very true. I think we all could see a little bit of ourselves in that."

He refuses to say any more about the article's contents, but from his conspiratorial smile it's clear that it must have been at least a little damaging.

We part on cordial terms, though no closer to any "strategy" about the water.

5

In the late afternoon I set out for the Parkers' house, Castellina. I pass Casabassa again, but now the house is locked up and shuttered. The van is still there; perhaps the Wenzels are having a nap. I notice that the heavy front gate, flanked by new brick pillars, is bolted and secured with a thick chain. And they have actually planted roses to grow on the wall of the house.

I imagine Wenzel, from a bird's perspective, as a little fluttering human shape desperately clinging to the earth, his hands dug deep into his flower bed while the winds of adversity hurl his body up in the air, trying to wrest him away from it.

I think about his cryptic allusion to the article about foreigners in Tuscany. I wonder what malicious truths it uncovered. We're a diverse group. The closer one looks, the more the differences become apparent. Some are rich, others merely scraping by. Some, like the journalist Franziska Pongratz, a reporter for *Der Spiegel*, have transformed their piles of stone into elegant showpieces for architectural magazines. They show up at odd times throughout the year; their swimming pools, lemon-yellow sports cars, and white linen clothes add bright accents to the muted colors of the landscape. At the other end of the spectrum are the hippies from East Germany who stay at Spazzavento, "swept by the wind," the highest of all the houses, without water or electricity. Different groupings of them arrive each summer; they build bonfires at night and play bongo drums whose sound carries across the valley.

At various intermediate points on the income scale are the academics, the doctors, and so forth, each regarding the others with suspicion.

What is it that all of us have in common?

After Casabassa, I turn right on the stony track that leads back up into the hills. It winds its way gradually upwards, alternating between open stretches in the hot afternoon sun and cool stretches in the shade of the woods. After about twenty minutes, Castellina comes into view high above the road, like a fortress. When I get closer, two figures appear at the parapet, and Libby's voice sails down: "Helloooooo!"

I shout back.

Ten minutes later, after another loop in the road, I see them again, this time waiting to greet me at their gate.

"Come in, come in!"

They've taken over the custom of shaking hands from their German acquaintances, but accompany the handshakes with a grin as if they found it rather silly. Richard has exchanged his work clothes for freshly pressed light blue slacks and shirt; Libby is wearing a Marks & Spencer dress, bright lipstick and perfume. In all this festiveness, there is a touch of make-believe that fills me with happy anticipation. It reminds me of when I was small, and my friends and I would dress up and pretend to be adults.

"You'll have to excuse us, we're in a terrible state! The dishwasher broke, and all our dishes were in there. I just got finished doing them by hand. And then Richard went down to light the stove to warm the *bomboloni*, and it sort of blew up. You can even see where it singed his eyebrows. Show her, Richard!"

They are both in their fifties but seem far younger. Libby is tall and striking, with flaming red hair and freckles. She has a ringing voice that makes it easy for her to call out above the heads of other people toward the seemingly abandoned post office windows, "Is there any hope of getting a stamp?" Richard is accustomed to being in Libby's shadow. He is taciturn, with skeptical blue eyes and bushy eyebrows. Years ago, when I came to Florence by myself, the two of them took me under their wing. I became attached to them with the devotion of an adolescent for a couple too young to be my parents. We bridged the age difference by resorting to utter childishness. Richard, in particular, could make me laugh at almost nothing, just by moving an eyebrow. We used to incite each other to giggles. Once I choked from laughter and horrible croaking sounds came out of me, so that I had to leave the table and run to the kitchen.

All this was a long time ago, but the way they both smile at me shows that the old days, and those croaking sounds, haven't been forgotten.

"Anyway," Libby says, "we're a bit disorganized. But never mind. Put your things up here, otherwise the cats will sit on them. Do you want to know how many cats we have now? Eleven! It's disgusting!"

Richard rolls his eyes and picks up a gray cat that is rubbing itself affectionately against his leg. "This is Smokey. He showed up about two months ago."

"He's beautiful," I agree.

Two cats are sleeping in a basket; a third looks down at us from the top of an armoire so high it's impossible to see how it could have gotten up there.

Libby is from London, Richard from a small town in Oregon. They met at Signora Fini's art school in Florence. They bought Castellina, the most ruined of all the houses, for a very small sum. While Libby took a job with a Florentine publisher, Richard began to rebuild the house from the bottom up, learning from books and from talking to local builders how to do each thing as he went along. The first time we visited them, they were living in a single room. We sat on the bed and drank *spumante*. Golden light drifted in through the arched window and fell onto neat stacks of rose-colored bricks. Already then, Richard had several cats. Now and then he'd pull a morsel of food from his pocket and hold it up high to show how the cats were able to stand up and take it gingerly from his fingers. One even climbed on his shoulder.

The house, saved from slipping down the hillside by a new, massive cement foundation, has become more and more splendid over the years—the windows and doors all arches, each room on a different level, each window framing a different view of the bluish-green landscape. Candles and kerosene lamps were replaced by a generator, and then an electric line was brought up the hill. Gradually the Parkers have surrounded themselves with comfort, acquiring furniture and all the appliances that make life pleasant and easy. When Libby's Scottish grandmother died, Libby inherited bone china and a Steinway, along with scraps of a social code honed in the colonies ("Forks ever, spoons never!"), and enough money so that they can now live modestly without working.

As I am ushered through the rooms, I notice no sign of the "terrible state" that Libby described. On the walls hang beautiful paintings: still-lifes and interiors in the style of the old masters. Everything is in its place and spotless. I suspect that Libby's way of exaggerating things, giving them a twist of absurdity, also comes from her Granny. She once showed me the silver beaker used by her grandfather when he was a tax collector in Burma. Granny visited Libby and Richard in the Mugello until she was ninety-seven, effortlessly adapting from Burma to Italy. Any Italian crossing the road in front of the car was simply "Charlie."

"What about the studio?" I ask. "Can I see it?"

The painting studio at the top of the house was left to the last. Even after it was built, it was used to store supplies while the other rooms were brought to perfection.

"It's not finished yet."

"Oh, come on, Richard," says Libby.

"Please."

But Richard remains stubborn.

"Richard, you know you're going to have to try to light that stove again."

Richard obeys, throwing me a look. "I'll wave to you in passing if it blows up again."

We sit on the terrace under a striped awning. The *bomboloni* are filled with custard or jam that spills out on either side when you bite into them. There are plenty of napkins. It's very quiet. The wooded hills around the house give way to a view of the valley from a different angle than Querceto's. Once in a long while, you can hear a car coming up the road, and then Richard gets up quickly to see who it is.

"We're getting more and more traffic up here, it's terrible!" Libby cries out into the stillness. "The dust these cars raise! They go much too fast!"

At a certain point in the road there is a larger than usual bump. When Richard sees a car coming too fast, he waits at the parapet to see if it will "hit bottom" on the bump. With any luck it will do it twice.

I wonder what traffic there could possibly be on this road that leads nowhere except to Spazzavento and another small house, La Roccia, where the Mandelbaums live.

"All kinds of people," Libby says. "Wood-cutters. Hunters in the fall, of course, and people looking for mushrooms, or just exploring. The road goes on for quite a bit beyond La Roccia. There's a Sicilian who has bought a little piece of land up there and put a trailer on it. It's a real eyesore. He's always driving up and down the hill. Sometimes he gets drunk and makes a lot of noise."

Richard sits down again after a car has hit bottom very satisfactorily, twice.

"He has a bunch of cows that he lets roam loose, terrorizing the countryside. They've been trampling through people's gardens and eating their plants. One of them recently got its head stuck in a bucket. It was last seen wandering toward a precipice. Renato came in the nick of time to save it.

"And just the other day, one of the bulls ran at a woman down in Cetinale. She wasn't hurt, but she fainted. People have started calling the municipal authorities to try to get the cows stopped. Now the *carabinieri* have given the Sicilian an ultimatum: either he gets rid of them or they will be taken away from him."

Libby and Richard regale me with stories about their Mugello neighbors. They know almost everyone. Libby's sociable nature converts the seasonal flotsam of foreigners into a loose community where dinner invitations are given and received in a rotating continuum. Hardly have one group left for the year than it's time for another to arrive. The winter offers a lull of several months, giving the Parkers time to recall everything that was said during each of the dinner parties, so that they can pick up conversations a year later as if no time had passed, and find amusement in the blank faces of their guests, who often cannot remember their own anecdotes.

I tell them about my meeting with the Wenzels.

"He probably didn't realize," says Richard, "that her foot was caught in the car door and was dragging on the highway the whole way."

Libby and Richard have never met the Wenzels, but Libby has heard a story about Frau Wenzel from a man named Squilloni, who heard it from the builders who installed the Wenzels' septic tank. The builders had to get down into the newly installed septic tank, and asked their employers not to use the toilet for the next hour.

"Frau Wenzel either didn't understand the instructions or forgot. And she *went*! Isn't it awful? She's become known for it throughout the area, although she is probably unaware of her fame."

"That reminds me," says Richard, "of a time when we were invited to a party. There was this lovely arbor of grape vines shading the table in the garden. The grapes were ripe. One of the other guests, on a visit from Hamburg, I believe, picked a grape and ate it. 'This is fantastic!' he exclaimed. So sweet, so juicy, he had never tasted grapes so good; and he picked one after the other and stuffed them in his mouth. I told him: 'That's because they're growing over the septic tank.' A look of horror came over the man's face, and the next moment he lurched forward and spat out his whole mouthful of grapes."

"I think," says Libby, "that there's a book called, *The Grass is Always Greener Over the Septic Tank*."

I end up staying for dinner. The sun goes down and in the dusk the hills seem to huddle more closely around the house. Bats appear. At first glance they look like swallows, but they fly differently, with sudden sharp turns and reversals. Finally, Richard brings up the subject that has been weighing on my mind all evening.

"I hear you don't have any water."

"None. The cisterns are dry. Landi is going to bring me some tomorrow, to tide me over. But I can't afford to keep doing that. – It's very strange," I add, "when I brought it up with the Donatis, I had the impression they knew something more than they were willing to tell me. First Costanzo said it was the drought, and then he said it was the Cavinis."

I immediately regret having said this. It seems disloyal to have any kind of suspicion about Costanzo and Silvana.

"The Cavinis only come on the weekends, don't they?" I continue quickly. "But the Wenzels say they haven't had any water all week."

I passed the Cavinis' house, Pruneto, on the way up; it was barely visible through all the trees they've planted around it.

"They were definitely here this weekend," says Richard, looking at Libby. "They had their laundry hung up all over the place."

"So they must have had water. Perhaps they have some kind of faucet that they've kept running, so there's none left to come down to us."

Richard proposes going immediately to look, but Libby holds him back. "Really, Richard, we can't just go prowling around their property when they're not home. Especially at night! I think Christine should ask Renato first, don't you? He's sure to know what's going on there." She adds decisively: "Talk to Renato. Talk to him tomorrow."

"What is your source of water?" It has never occurred to me to ask this before.

"Oh, we have our own well. It was here when we bought the house, and we've only had to dig it a little deeper."

I have the feeling Libby wants to dismiss the topic quickly.

After dessert, Richard insists on driving me home, waving aside my protests that I can walk. He drives very slowly and carefully, familiar with every bump in the road. The headlights pick out a tiny area from the surrounding darkness. At one point we stop short because there is a frog in our path. When it doesn't move, Richard gets out and gently carries it off to the side.

As we drive on, he reminds me of the reasons I have to be afraid to walk in the dark. There are poisonous vipers in the woods, which sometimes drop down from trees. And have I forgotten about the Monster of the Mugello?

"Really? They drop from trees?—Wasn't the Monster caught a few years ago?" I remember reading in the newspaper that the feared serial killer, who for over a decade had murdered and mutilated young couples in isolated places, turned out to be an elderly man, the innocent-looking type that one sees everywhere tending their vegetable gardens or playing cards. In fact, he had several other elderly men helping him. One of the headlines read: *A Cooperative of Monsters!*

"Yes, but he's been released. They let him go on a technicality. The whole thing was declared a mistrial. So you see—he could be at it again."

I smile and say nothing. We round the corner at Casabassa, and I tense as Richard switches into four-wheel drive. This last steep piece of road has huge rocks and ridges jutting out. It's almost impossible not to hit bottom. Yet Richard succeeds. At the top he positions the car so that the headlights shine on the front door.

I've just put my key in the lock when he yells: "Wait!"

In a second he is out of the car. I step back from the door. Following the line of his gaze, I see, curling above it on the stone lintel, a thin brown snake.

"Move back. Do you have a long stick or something?"

There are plenty of sticks lying around. A minute later, we are staring down at the corpse of the viper.

"Look at that," he says. "A big one. Are you sure you're going to be all right? You're not afraid to stay here by yourself?"

6

Landi shows up first thing in the morning, as promised. I hear his tractor before I see it coming out of the clump of woods that lies between Renato's farm and Querceto. The tractor is pulling a round metal tank.

I stand and watch as the tractor makes its steady progress up the hill from Casabassa. Landi sits in a relaxed position, looking calmly left and right, only not in my direction, like someone who is aware of making an entry. It's an excruciatingly slow entry, as the tank must be quite heavy. But the slowness has a certain dramatic value of its own.

It's not until he has maneuvered the tank into a position above the level of the cistern and turned off the tractor motor that he deigns to acknowledge me. Landi is a large silent man with a mop of brown hair that seems somehow strangely placed on his head. According to Libby, he works nights at a Fiat plant; that would explain his pale and scattered appearance. He customarily holds a reed or blade of grass in his mouth and has the air of an embarrassed adolescent, along with a smirk that I don't know how to interpret.

I like these things about him.

"You should use your well," is his advice.

It takes some minutes for the water to be transferred and there is no getting around conversation.

"But there's nothing in it. We tried it a long time ago."

We tried the well the first time water failed to come through the tube from the spring. I remember it took us a day just to clear away the brambles that had grown over it. Full of hope, we bought a new pulley and ropes and a bucket. But it turned out there were only a few inches of fetid yellowish muck at the bottom.

"Sure, there's water. Either there or in another place. Maybe you have to dig a little deeper."

"But how would we know for sure before digging?"

"I could call one of my friends who has the gift."

"The gift?"

"Yes, there are a few people who have the gift, maybe in their feet, I don't know. They use a pendulum or a divining rod."

He says that there are only two of them in the area, and the one he uses has never been wrong.

I must have shown my skepticism about these methods all too plainly, for Landi clams up defensively after that.

Later I think regretfully that my dismissal of the notion of diviners was probably a bit rude. An *idraulico*, in these parts, is not merely a plumber but an expert in water matters. But it seems absurd to drill into the earth on the basis of what's in someone's foot.

I now have enough water to last me a week or so, if I use it sparingly.

With the cisterns full, the sense of urgency that carried me through the first two days is suddenly gone. The day is still young. The sun is shining. The air is mild. A cock crows over at La Croce, which is wrapped in a delicate haze. The white mist that boils up from the valley in the mornings, sometimes reaching as high as Querceto but more often stopping just below, hasn't completely evaporated yet; there are still swaths of it lingering here and there.

I run upstairs and switch on the water heater in the bathroom. Then I begin unpacking more of my books, setting up my desk. Landi, too, asked me the same thing as Richard.

"You're here alone? You're not afraid?"

"No, I'm not afraid," I said, with a dismissive

smile.

A woman alone: how I hate this phrase, with its ominous suggestion of violence or at least incompleteness. Nobody gives it a second thought when a man goes off and does something on his own.

But the truth is that I'm a little worried. I've stayed here alone only once before, when I was seventeen. It was not a success. Then, too, I had simply wanted to be by myself. My mother didn't think it was a good idea; she was concerned about the isolation of the house, which at that time had no phone. She reminded me to be alert and to keep the doors locked when I was inside. And she gave me a gas-driven siren in case of an emergency.

With these warnings in mind, I went a little crazy. In the evenings, I'd lock myself in as soon as dusk fell. When I went to bed, I would start to hear noises in the silence of the house. I'd hear the would-be intruder filing away at the lock of the door downstairs, or probing for a foothold as he scrambled up the rough fieldstone walls. Or perhaps he had already made his way inside, and those were the little bones in his feet crackling as he tiptoed through the next room...

La Croce was too far away for comfort. Even if Costanzo and Silvana heard my siren, what could they do? Casabassa, at that time, was empty.

During the first two days, not a single car passed by Querceto. The only sign of life was a shepherd with his flock on a distant hill. I watched them through my binoculars, and occasionally the faint tinkling of the sheep's bells or a brief shout would reach me across the valley. But on the third morning I was awakened by the sound of bells quite close, and when I pushed open the shutters I saw that the shepherd and his flock were at the bottom of the hill. Just at that moment, he glanced up toward the house. He undoubtedly remarked the open window.

That day was my worst. I left all the windows closed except for the one I had already opened. Standing in the shadows so that he could not see my silhouette, I watched him make his way slowly up the hill. Through my binoculars, I could now see him as clearly as if he were standing before me. He was a lean, tall man, sunburnt, with a small shaven head. He looked completely unlike the bearded, contemplative shepherds with floppy hats one sees depicted. There was an air of brutality about him.

He scarcely glanced up at the house again after that first, direct look: as if that had been enough, as if he knew now that I was inside. But he kept coming closer, moving steadily up the hill along with his flock of sheep. Those sheep, inseparable from the man, gave him a terrible power, like an evil gray tide rising toward the house.

A little after noon, the sheep reached Querceto and began to pour all around it. I could now hear their bells from every direction. The shepherd stopped on our terrace right beneath the window I had opened. I stood trembling, pressed against the wall, but unable to stop myself from peeking out to see what he was doing. Looking up directly for the second time, he opened his trousers and urinated against the side of the house.

After this he followed his sheep around to the other side and on toward La Croce. I was ecstatic. I laughed and ran from room to room for joy. The shepherd's rude gesture had reassured me completely. It was nothing but a message of defiance, intended to assert his territorial rights. Probably he had grazed his sheep on that terrain for many years and was not about to let some foreigner cause problems for him.

The rest of my stay passed uneventfully. My fear abated somewhat. But a year or two later, we heard a story that justified my impression of the shepherd. In a drunken rage, he had hit Franca, Mario's wife, on the head with a wine bottle, injuring her so severely that she had to be rushed to the hospital.

We'd see him once in a while, sometimes near the Villa, more often as a small figure in the distance. He was known only as *il Sardo*, "the Sardinian." I haven't seen him in many years.

Anyway, I'm older now. And the house does have a telephone.

7

My first awareness on waking up from a nap is of the sweet smell of the irises I have cut and put in a vase on the marble-topped dresser. I turn on my side to look at them. They are gigantic, standing on three-foot stems. The blossoms seem to glow in the semi-darkness, with yellow stamens crawling out of their centers like caterpillars. A large fly is buzzing around the room; it must have woken me up. I think about getting up to open the window or to find the plastic fly swatter that must be lying around somewhere. But then I am too lazy to move, and decide just to let it be. What determines its course? Is it systematically exploring the space, or is it just randomly shooting about, dashing itself against the windowpane by accident, and then flying away again unaffected?

Now it seems to be settling down, stopping more frequently and longer. It alights on the side of the dresser. The old wood varnish has a spotty, silvery sheen to it, and the silvery fly is less visible than its darker shadow making angular turns this way and that. The fly suddenly seems as beautiful to me as the flowers.

In reality, the house is not empty. It is full of the

creatures which are its only inhabitants throughout most of the year, creatures whose natural element is silence. Spiders and centipedes. Delicate moths that come in the night, attracted by the one lamp I leave burning. The bright emerald thing on my bath towel this morning. The pipe-cleaner worm, thick and fuzzy, moving rapidly along the edge of the wall.

I am always startled by these insect encounters. You don't expect them, and suddenly there they are. The silence is like a lens, it magnifies things. Time stops for a moment. There is a feeling of words unspoken. Often I'll say something out loud — something silly like "Oh! What's this?" — to reassure myself. Some of the creatures are so strange looking that they seem highly individual, as if there couldn't possibly exist another being remotely like them in the world.

As I am talking to Libby on the phone, thanking her for dinner, I see a scorpion on the threshold of the door. It's a medium-sized one, larger than the one I saw crawling along the frame of the *stallina* door when I opened it for Landi. Tied to the phone, I am too far away to step on it. I lose sight of it for a few moments. Then, as I absent-mindedly move the door a little bit with my foot, I see it drop to the ground from somewhere higher up. It scuttles away into a hole. There are two holes side by side, the same size, like a front and back entrance. I wish I knew how to lure it out, what little tidbit would be so irresistible to a scorpion that it would venture forth to its doom.

These creatures must adapt themselves to my presence. As I brush the crumbs from my plate onto the terrace, I almost feel sorry, knowing that the ants will have to labor for hours to carry them away, that they can't stop until the stones are clean.

I've just begun to look over the notes I made years ago when a motor starts up at close quarters behind the house. I go to look out the window. Silvana and Costanzo are on the terrace below. They've come to cut the grass. I didn't ask them to do this. Costanzo has a huge machine strapped to his back, equipped with its own gas tank. I wonder if it's the kind he uses on his highway job. I run downstairs and vainly shout, "*Basta!* It's not necessary!" My voice can barely be heard above the din of the grass-cutter. Costanzo is bent over and breathing heavily under its weight. Silvana has a little sickle in her hand with which she makes pecking, hacking motions.

"It's like me," she says, holding the sickle up with a laugh, "old and good for nothing."

"Please stop. I can do it myself."

This grass-cutting is part of an arrangement made in the very beginning between my parents and the Donatis. Silvana and Costanzo did small caretaking tasks in return for the hay from our field and the use of the bake house to store it. The notary had explained to my parents that there had to be a quid-pro-quo, if not in money, then in service; otherwise the field would become theirs after twelve years through the law of usucaption.

Now this arrangement seems hopelessly outdated, especially since Renato took over the hay field some years back. Perhaps they passed it on to him in another quid-pro-quo. In any case, I belong to the next generation: the whole thing has nothing to do with me. It embarrasses me.

I beg them to stop, but my entreaties are ignored. If anything, they seem to cheer them on. Costanzo, as the machine-bearer, likes having Silvana in attendance. He periodically orders her to brush the grass from the bottoms of his corduroy trousers. At one point, when she has wandered off in the opposite direction with her sickle, he stops the machine.

"Hey! Where's Silvana? Tell her to come over here!" He panics at being left alone in my presence. He feels lost if he's without her for even a minute. I realize he is lording it over her to save face. When she comes, smiling at me in apology for his rudeness, he tells her to clean out the grass that has accumulated in the blades of his machine. She pokes at the blades with the tip of her sickle.

"Take it out with your hands." He can't do it himself with the machine strapped to his back.

"I'm afraid."

"Don't be afraid, just grab it with your hands!"

She continues to scrape ineffectually with the sickle.

"With your hands!"

Finally she gives in and cleans the blades with her hands.

Afterward, they consent to come into the kitchen for some refreshment. They accept no wine or juice, but only half a glass of water each, sitting on the edges of their chairs and sipping it cautiously, because refrigerated water is dangerous for your health.

In the late afternoon I sit on the terrace reading. At the bottom of the hill I see a spot of flesh color among the olive trees: Giorgi, bare to the waist, working in his garden. He is an in-law of Costanzo's who has bought himself a tiny patch of land next to Casabassa. How does he water his plants?

A few feet from where I am sitting, a lizard rests motionless on the sunny stone, undisturbed by an ant that is exploring its splayed foot, toe by toe. The lizard is so neat and precise, as if enameled, emerald with a black design.

Suddenly I hear a male voice coming from the right side of the house, behind me. It sounds quite close by. When I turn around to try to determine its provenance, the lizard is gone in a flash.

I can tell it's a German voice: probably Wenzel, I think, taking a walk with his wife. But the voice seems to be stationary. After a while, I hear a second male voice, less loud and curiously squawky, responding. Are they going to come this way? I wait. Then, as the voices still seem to be staying in the same place, I get up to have a look.

I finally realize what I've been hearing. It's Klaus Ziegmann, "Claudio" as he calls himself here, the philosophy professor who owns one of the two houses below Renato's farm. He is sitting under our big oak tree, dressed in cherry-red overalls, speaking into a dictating machine. Now I recognize the droning cadence and hollow intonation of academic prose, complete with punctuation marks. "Blablabla, *Komma*, blabla, *Komma*, blablablabla, *Punkt*." After every couple of phrases he plays back to himself what he has just said, so that he can finish his sentence correctly.

He pretends not to see me and I'm glad, I run into the house, doubled over with laughter. He takes the opportunity of my being inside to make his getaway, as he thinks, unseen. But I watch him from one of the upstairs windows as he goes slowly down the hill, still finishing his thought, finally tucking the recorder into the bib of his overalls. I watch him for a long time, walking stiffly down the empty, dusty path, a lonely spot of red, until the trees swallow him up.

Now it strikes me: that odd little bench I found on the terrace, that looks as if it had been hammered together by a child — it must be his. He must have used our terrace to do his thinking and his dictating. I've displaced him from his spot.

When Costanzo asked me how long I was going to stay, I said, "as long as possible," and thought nothing of it. Now I realize it's not only the insects that are being disturbed by my presence. My arrival must have sent shock waves spreading through the landscape. A silent alarm has gone out; adjustments are being made. Someone must have found a new place to tether the horse whose droppings under the loggia were still fresh when I arrived. And I notice that some tools left by the side of the house have disappeared overnight.

8

I check the cisterns several times a day. I am obsessed with making Landi's water last as long as possible. I use a ruler to measure how much the level has gone down. I still use bottled water for washing my face, and fruits and vegetables. I've devised a method of holding the bottle in the crook of my left arm so that both my hands are free. By leaning forward just a little, I can make it pour out as from a spout. When I wash dishes, I save the water and pour it into a bucket, which I carry upstairs and re-use for flushing the toilet. In a perverse way I enjoy these stratagems. It's as if I were playing a game, inventing the rules as I go along.

I think about Landi's statement that we should use our well, or dig a new one. I don't set much store by this idea. Why invest in such a dubious enterprise when we already have a spring? Or at least a third of one, or a fourth if Renato's shed across from Casabassa is counted. And it certainly should be counted, since there are, even now, three or four cows in it. The trough, I noticed, was filled.

Why isn't water coming to Querceto or Casabassa? Renato would be pleased if we dug a well and gave up on the spring. More water for his cattle.

But the spring is ours, too. There was always enough to go around, even when there were ten or twenty people living in each of the houses.

I know I have to talk to Renato. But I'm putting it off. The thought of it makes me apprehensive. We used to be on friendlier terms with him. In the old days, we used to take the main unpaved road to Querceto, which led from the Villa at the entrance of the estate past his farm. We'd stop to say hello to whoever was out in the yard; sometimes my parents would accept a *gocciolino*—a "droplet" of wine—and chat for a while. But when the last steep stretch of road climbing up from Casabassa deteriorated to the point where a normal car could no longer attempt it, we began to take a back route through the village of Cetinale. Thus the natural means of maintaining contact was gone.

That little piece of road between Casabassa and Querceto is a sore point. My parents used to have it repaired every couple of years. The last time, they went all out. On our builder's advice, they had cement channels laid across it at regular intervals so that the rainwater would go off to the side instead of making deep furrows between the rocks. It seemed like a good idea at the time. Each channel had a metal grating over it to prevent stones and dirt from falling in. But the gratings had no chance with Renato's big tractors and the lumber trucks he commissions. They were squashed down almost immediately. The channels became clogged, the rain washed away the earth around them, and the road was left worse than before. Now there are foot-high cement ridges jutting up above the rest of its surface.

My brother takes a hard line, and I agree with him. Renato uses the road more than anyone else. His tractors and trucks ruin it. He should take care of it. I've always liked Renato, but now he is angry at us. It was very convenient for him to have us repairing the road.

In the early days, we didn't even know that the road through Cetinale, which passes the farms of Riaccio and La Croce, existed. We thought that the road winding up from the Villa was the only way to get to Querceto.

One summer, we heard a story about a man who lived at Riaccio, a man we had never met named Lodovico. Lodovico, this was how the story went, had gone chestnut gathering up in the woods one day with his brother's wife. When they came back, Lodovico's brother's wife moved into Lodovico's house. Lodovico gave his brother a herd of sheep, and the two brothers were reconciled.

The gossip arising out of this scandal reached even our ears.

"A whole herd of sheep, that's really something." Renato squinted appraisingly. "That means at least two hundred animals, you know."

We knew that the figure was not to be taken too literally; two hundred was a standard estimate with the peasants. Their houses were "maybe two hundred" years old, any distant city "about two hundred" kilometers away. Still, a herd of sheep was impressive, a small livelihood. Not, as Renato pointed out, something one could take care of on the side, like a few olive trees or a vegetable garden. You needed dogs, and facilities for making and storing the cheese.

Renato's tone was completely serious. "And it's not easy, making a good cheese!"

The incident must have been an embarrassment. No one knew quite what to say about it.

"Yes, that's right, they went alone, the two of them." Renato's wife Alessandra rubbed her palms on the sides of her housedress in an instinctive gesture of cleaning them off for conversation. "There was nobody else." Her eyes were bright, and she was silent for a moment. "All in all," she said with a sudden grin, her gold tooth shining like a small treasure, "when they came back, they were a couple."

Silvana was angry. "That woman is not from here. She's from the South. Well, yes, it's true," conceding Costanzo's muttered correction, "she'd been living in Pontassieve. But they say she has an accent. I don't even remember her name. I've heard she's not—perhaps not very serious. While they were engaged, he didn't bring her home very often; that's why we still hardly know her. Oh, no, I'm sure she's not a bad woman. She works hard on the field. Who knows..." The next moment her face resumed its usual expression. She laughed apologetically. "Let's talk about something else."

The chorus seemed to divide itself into two groups, those who were appalled and those who were intrigued. But it was only the woman who was discussed at all. The nature of the exchange that had taken place didn't seem to bother anyone. Lodovico and his brother were simply too familiar to be talked about. The two of them had always gotten on well together.

"You see," Costanzo said, "even now, they had a problem between them, and they solved it in this way. A herd of sheep is no small thing, you know."

It turned out that when the woman had moved from one house to the other she hadn't had very far to go, as the two houses were adjoining. I saw Riaccio for the first time from the back of the Parkers' car, the following year. They had taken me on an outing, and we came back by way of Cetinale.

"You'll see where Lodovico and his brother live," Libby said. "It's coming up now on the right, around this bend. There, there it is."

We passed the farm slowly, two buildings connected by a third, forming a kind of courtyard. But I didn't take in the details of the architecture: all I saw was the pigs. There were pigs everywhere, pigs lying on their sides or bellies, pigs oozing out of doorways and openings, pigs conglomerated, draped over each other. They were napping in the midday heat. Wherever one looked, there was another whitish, pinkish body stretched out in the shade of a bench or rolled up by the side of a wall.

It was as if the whole herd of sheep given in exchange for the wife had been metamorphosed into pigs.

"And there's Lodovico!" We saw him on the other side of the road in his field, bathed in full sunlight. He had heard us coming and was leaning on his hoe to watch us pass by. Richard honked, and

Lodovico raised his hand in greeting. As he turned his head after us I could see that he wore the strangest expression, a mixture of astonishment and amusement and joy. It was as if, so far from feeling himself an object of curiosity, he found us one of the more entertaining sights to have come his way in a while.

Although I've taken the Cetinale road many times since then, it still has the feel of a strange foreign world. The people at Riaccio look wild and uncouth, completely different from Renato and his family. The notion of stopping to chat is out of the question. The pigs are gone, but there are other animals: those dogs that run after the car, and stray cats, chickens, sometimes a horse or two.

The farm itself is half in ruins. Once, glancing up briefly as I was being chased by the dogs, I saw a goat standing sideways, in profile, in the dark opening of a second-floor window, with only a scrap of wire mesh to prevent it from plunging down.

9

Silvana insisted that I come visit them again this evening.

After we've been talking for a while, she suddenly gets up and disappears into the back room. She never brings out refreshments right away. She waits for a certain amount of time, acting as if she had no intention of offering anything. It's only after one has given up hope that she goes to fetch wine and water and a plate of irregularly cut strips of yellow cake. The cake is fresh and fragrant, still warm from the oven. I wonder if this way of presenting it, in haphazardly hacked pieces like leftovers, is a form of modesty, a way of saying, "Here is my cake—it's nothing special."

As always, I decline the wine, then agree to have just a drop in my water, "for color." They smile their approval. I do everything to distinguish myself from the other foreigners, who are known to "drink a little." Silvana dilutes hers as well, sipping with the concentration of a child tasting wine for the first time.

She must have baked the cake specially for me. I take a second piece and praise it extravagantly. It really is light and delicious.

Costanzo refuses it: "I don't eat sweets." He

lights up a cigarette instead, with a defiant air.

"He always smokes," Silvana complains. "The doctors say he should stop smoking. He'll get emphysema—what am I saying? He practically has it already! But he doesn't listen. He keeps on smoking. If anything, he's smoking even more now."

"That's not true." Costanzo looks at me from the corner of his eye. He flicks his cigarette ash on the floor. I have entered a realm governed by infinite politeness and almost otherworldly delicacy on the one hand and strangely crude habits on the other. The rules are simply different.

I ask Costanzo how he is feeling.

"Better. I'm better," he replies curtly. "How many people live in New York?" he wants to know, changing the subject.

I have no idea.

I always feel guilty when I see Costanzo and Silvana again after an interval. Perhaps it's simply that I have left while they remained here. We foreigners move freely, we come and go; they are forced to welcome us whenever we return.

Silvana has never been to Rome or Venice. In fact, she's never been farther away than Florence. Costanzo, on the other hand, did his military service in Genoa. He's seen something of the world. He has a sense of relativity. As in an old-fashioned geography lesson, he produces figures, statistics. He knows by heart the populations of Italy, Germany, Russia, and America; though he's not sure, he might have Russia and America mixed up.

Costanzo's insistence on these stylized topics is at once more sophisticated and more simpleminded than Silvana's straightforward approach. He senses the need to strike a pose. He has observed in others the practice of a separate form of "conversation with foreigners." Unlike Silvana, who doesn't aspire to worldliness, he doesn't instinctively recognize its absurdity.

Costanzo has had a hard life. As a boy he learned from his father the craft of a *carbonaio*, making charcoal by burning wood very slowly in fires constructed a certain way. By the time he was an adult, this profession was already obsolete. After the military he worked for a while as a woodcutter. He probably felt lucky to get the job with the national highway maintenance, ANAS. You see those crews by the side of the road, unprotected from the broiling sun, cutting the parched grass and dusty shrubs in a haze of automobile fumes. But it's a government job, a steady salary, days off, and a pension to look forward to. This has been his living for forty years. He comes home at two, sleeps, then works in his vegetable plot.

I remember how he used to let us children climb on his horse, taught us how to dig up potatoes with a hoe, chuckling at our clumsiness. There's something about his aspect that has changed. It's not just that he is older—he still has his full head of hair, and he has a new set of teeth, as Silvana repeatedly points out. I can't put my finger on what it is.

We talk about this and that. But our conversation is awkward tonight. It's what's unspoken: none of us have mentioned the water. They know I've had to buy it from Landi. Why aren't they asking me about it?

"I saw Giorgi working in his garden," I blurt out suddenly. I have no idea what his first name is; although he's a relative of theirs, they only refer to him as Giorgi. "It's strange, there's no water at Querceto or Casabassa, yet he seems to have it."

Both Costanzo and Silvana rush to tell me that he gets his water from a completely different source. "His comes from over here, from La Croce," they say. "It doesn't come from your spring." Even Silvana is emphatic.

My behavior makes me cringe in retrospect. I knock my wine glass over. I am sitting on the little bench, my legs crossed; I am holding the glass on my knee with one hand and tilt it with a careless gesture of the other. The watered-down wine spills on my pants and onto the floor. I am not so much embarrassed by this accident as I welcome the opportunity to throw myself into exaggerated apologies and self-deprecation. I even refuse to wipe off my pants, saying that they are "ugly" anyway.

I want to make amends for having suspected Giorgi.

In the morning, the water level in the cisterns has gone down by thirty centimeters.

It's an overcast, misty day. Renato's cattle, on the field below the bake house, are making deep sounds like foghorns. The temperature is still mild, and then the clouds pull away without giving any rain. Sitting at my desk, I hear Silvana's voice over at La Croce, the constant clinking of cowbells, and a cuckoo. The cows stay immobile, only their ears flapping back and forth occasionally and their tails twitching slightly, their jaws moving.

Earlier, a car at La Croce had trouble starting; then, after it drove off, I heard a mockingbird make exactly that same noise, like a car that won't turn over.

I take a walk down to Casabassa. I have a notion of asking Wenzel to accompany me on my visit to Renato. But the house is all shuttered up. The wicker chairs have disappeared from the graveled patio. Of course, they have left for Germany again. I feel disappointed. He didn't even say goodbye. What about our plans to do something about the water jointly? All eagerness one day, gone the next. What about digging your claws into the earth?

10

Renato's handshake is dry and light and returns no pressure. It's like touching a piece of balsa wood.

He knows exactly what the problem is. "It was the storm. The tube must be broken." Seeing my dumbfounded expression, he clarifies: "There was a big storm in the spring, before you came. In April. It did a lot of damage, broken branches, even whole trees. It must have carried away the tube."

Standing near the front door, Alessandra waves at me, half turned away as if only pausing for a moment in her work. Ordinarily she might come and greet me, but it is obvious that my visit is for business, not pleasure. In her fifties, she is still strikingly lovely, with large, wide-spaced eyes. I can't help noticing how well-tended everything is here, down to the patch of English lawn and the flower bed in front. They've been renovating the house. According to Libby, they have been redoing it on the inside as well, in preparation for Lorenzo getting married. Libby has seen the new bathrooms, which she says are "nicer than at the Savoy."

"The tube? But isn't it mostly underground?" I remember that when my parents had a new line put in,

77

the largest part of the expense was to dig a twenty-centimeter ditch the entire length of it so that it could be safely buried.

"Not that tube. The tube that leads to the spring."

"How... that leads to the spring?"

"Yes, the tube that leads from the river to the spring." Renato enunciates clearly, in his special loud voice for foreigners. He is a head shorter than me, sunburnt, with a large beak nose and a baseball cap.

I mentally review the crucial vocabulary. *Sorgente* = spring. *Fiume* = river. There is no river anywhere nearby. Unnerved, I stumble over my words. "Isn't the *sorgente* the place where the water comes out of the ground?"

"Yes, yes." Renato laughs indulgently at my confusion. He explains that because so many people are now attached to the spring, there is no longer enough water to go around. So they've put a tube down the hill, where there is a stream, to replenish the spring. That is the one that the storm must have dislodged.

As he is speaking, Lorenzo passes by, acknowledging me with a nod. He is good-looking; he resembles his mother. His thick curls look oddly mottled in the brief moment I glimpse him, perhaps whitened by dust from his work. Over Renato's shoulder, I see Alessandra, still watching and listening to our conversation with an expression of undissimulated intelligence. It occurs to me that one ought always to look at Alessandra while listening to Renato, that together they make the whole picture.

Renato sees that I am unconvinced. "It's Elisabetta's fault that the spring is running dry," he says challengingly. "Elisabetta" is Libby. It is common to refer to a couple by its more prominent member, though in Italy this would ordinarily be the man. "She taps into it above everyone else, so she gets the water first. It's *our* water she's using."

"But they have a well..."

"Her well taps into our spring. It's because of her that there isn't enough to go around."

He is well aware that we are friends.

"Believe me, that's the way it is. It's Elisabetta's fault. I'll tell you what," he offers. "We'll go with Landi to look at the tube. This afternoon. We'll go at six. *Va bene?*"

Walking home, I reflect on our conversation. I know nothing about hydrology, but it doesn't seem right that the output of a spring should depend on a rubber tube feeding it from a trickling mountain rivulet. And what about the Parkers' well tapping into

79

our spring? I suppose it's possible. But even if it were true, what could one do about it? It seems fruitless to speculate about what goes on below the earth.

Back at Querceto, I call Libby. I tell her about Renato's accusation with a laugh, having decided to discount it.

"Renato *lies*," she says angrily. "Everyone knows Renato is *furbo*. He's crafty. You should ask Franziska about him. He shares a water line with her, and she's *sure* he's diverting some of her water. But she knows how to deal with him. She's a tough woman, you know."

She says it is common knowledge that when Renato organizes a consortium to pay for road repairs, he always manages it so that the foreigners pay for everything and he never has to pay a lira.

Renato and Landi pick me up at the fork in the road below Casabassa. Landi is driving; it must be his car. I get into the back seat. After our exchanged greetings, silence falls. I consider various conversational openings and dismiss them. Perhaps there is an impropriety in my going alone with these two men? In Italy, women talk to women and men talk to men. I console myself with the thought that in any case they probably hardly see me as a woman. They see me as a *tedesca*, a German; smile about me behind my back the way they smile about Frau Wenzel. Perhaps they will come to see me as a "tough woman," like Franziska or Libby. I grin inwardly: why not?

Libby has told me how, years ago, Renato's mother used to address questioning looks at her while stroking her belly. Then one day Libby overheard her telling someone, "She's not fertile." – But they have learned to reckon with Libby.

Once in a while, Renato mutters something to Landi, who responds with a grunt. They are probably commenting on the state of a field or the condition of the olive trees. To me the landscape is all beautiful; it hardly makes a difference to my perception if there has been drought or rain. What they see is completely different. They know each piece intimately and individually.

We drive up past Pruneto, hidden in its trees and shrubbery, and Castellina, where the Parkers' striped awning is fluttering in the wind. At the fork where the road ascends toward Spazzavento on the left, Landi turns right. About fifty meters into the woods, he stops and turns off the motor. Still neither of them has said a word to me. I put on a businesslike face as I get out of the car, but underneath I feel a happy excitement, like a child being taken on an outing. In silence and single-file, we tramp down into the underbrush. The Cavinis' house and the spring must be somewhere below.

We come to a little stream. Landi picks up a long stick and begins poking around in the leaves and rocks that fill the stream bed with the look of someone who knows what he is doing.

Renato stands next to me. He gazes about him with an appraising air.

"Look at that. The storm did that, and that. *Madonna*."

Large branches have been broken off the trees. In some cases, you can tell which tree they were torn from by matching the jagged edges.

Meanwhile, Landi has moved a little further downstream, still poking in the leaves.

"A big storm!" Renato says loudly, making a sweeping gesture with his arm. "In April!"

"Yes, yes, I understood that." I feel annoyed. From one moment to the next, people will forget that you were just having a normal conversation and begin shouting at you as if you were an imbecile. At least Costanzo and Silvana never do that. Costanzo has taken to saying, "She speaks just like us." Although I know it isn't true, I am still vain about my Italian.

We are following Landi at a respectful distance. "There's not much water in the river." Renato is pointing to a place where the little stream disappears for a moment beneath some rocks. Then, with the force of a statement saved up for the right moment: "You should use your well!"

"We have always gotten our water from the spring," I reply coldly, swallowing the anger that mounts in me. Is that what this charade is about?

"There must be some water in it," I add. "The Cavinis did their laundry on the weekend, and yet Querceto and Casabassa haven't had any water. Perhaps they've turned it off on us."

At this moment, Landi says, "I found it."

He is holding up a thin black rubber tube. We watch as he begins tugging at it, moving it this way and that, following its course with his eyes, removing a branch here, a stone there.

"It's not broken," he says. He finally draws himself up. "Now, let's see." He looks pleased, as with a job well done. He says something very quickly to Renato in an undertone, and Renato turns to me and says, "Now go up to Querceto and see if the water isn't coming in. Wait an hour."

I tell them I prefer to walk back, for exercise. The

car rumbles off down the path; I am glad to be alone. A few minutes later I hear a thud and feel a surge of joy—they hit bottom!

I don't for a minute believe that Landi's maneuvering will restore water to Querceto. And then what?

I realize that ever since Libby told me, "Ask Renato, he'll know," I've been pinning my hopes on him. I feel doubly disappointed, because secretly I had hoped not only that he would help me, but that somehow the friendly relations between us could be restored in the process.

I walk past the Parkers' house without stopping. I think to myself that they are probably enjoying their *aperitivi* on the terrace right now, smug with their well that never goes dry, that taps into sources mysteriously replenished even in the hottest, driest summers. I picture them as if surrounded by cool, sparkling reservoirs, across which they will never hear my cries of distress.

I pass by Pruneto. Perhaps because I've never met the Cavinis, it's easy to direct my suspicion against them. Bringing their dirty laundry! These are boors who have converted their farmhouse into a "country cottage," with ornate shutters and brick gate posts whose sheer ugliness, much more than the sign *Attenti al Cane,* makes you want to stay out. I'm sure they must have some kind of valve which allows them to turn the water off on the houses below. One doesn't even have to assume there is any malice involved. Querceto and Casabassa stand empty for so much of the year; it would be understandable if they had gotten into the habit of keeping the valve closed to maximize their water supply.

But in that case, why did Renato avoid blaming them? Since he uses the water at Casabassa for his cattle, surely he would protest if they kept the valve shut.

A moment earlier, the solution seemed obvious, and I thought the whole matter could be resolved with a phone call. Now my certainty flags again. A sense of hopelessness comes over me. I am not going to be able to stay much longer.

Later in the evening, as I am eating my supper on the terrace, a sound is added to the silence that is subtler than a lizard moving through the grass, and yet sounds very loud in my ear. It is the dripping of water into the cistern.

11

The drops add up, and by morning the cisterns are full. Over the next days, I find that if I have a leisurely bath and don't re-use the dishwashing water for the toilet, I go through a third of the cisterns in a single day. Yet with the trickle continuing, they are always full again in the morning.

I don't understand what happened. I can't bring myself to believe that Landi's moving the tube around is what made the water return. But there is no doubt that one way or another, Renato is responsible.

The Donatis' reaction to my good news is interesting. "That's good, that's good," they say, and quickly change the subject. Costanzo has a lingering thoughtful look in his eyes as if he were pondering something.

I tell the Parkers about my expedition with Renato and Landi.

"That sounds pretty fishy to me," Richard remarks. "I think he gave you a little show, and then he and Landi went and turned on a faucet somewhere."

I am sitting once again on their terrace. We are having tea and ice cream. The main purpose of their capacious freezer seems to be to keep on hand as many different varieties of ice cream as possible. They even have individually wrapped confections, the kind you can buy in bars, with names like *Rolling Bon* and *Magnum*. The cookie in the *Rolling Bon* is bare on one side, chocolate-coated on the other, as if to prevent boredom from arising. The *Cornetto* reserves its surprise to the very last, a frozen lump of chocolate at the bottom of the cone that dissolves into a syrup in your mouth.

"Well, Renato came through at any rate," Libby says. "Didn't I tell you he would? So there you are."

Her anger at him seems to have melted away like the chocolate at the bottom of the *Cornetto*. She is at pains to correct her former statements. "Perhaps there was more to it than met the eye, but what do you care? We've always been on friendly terms with Renato. Of course it's true that he's *furbo*. But you can't really blame people for looking after their own interests, can you?"

"What about the Cavinis?" I suggest. "They must have a valve somewhere. Maybe Renato turned that."

But Libby and Richard both shake their heads.

Renato is not on speaking terms with Cavini, who treats all the peasants with contempt.

"Do you know what Cavini does? He's a postman! We went down to his house once because of some question about the electricity. He must have been having a party—we could hear the noise all the way up the road. When we knocked on the door, it suddenly went dead quiet. We knocked again, but no one answered. We think the reason is he'd invited his postman friends, they'd left work early, and were afraid of being caught off-duty. It was only eleven in the morning on a Saturday. Can't you just see it, all those postmen hiding inside the house, in their blue uniforms?"

"They're not the only ones," says Richard, "who hide inside the house."

"Oh, well," Libby retorts, laughing, "that's different. You see, we had Jehova's Witnesses bothering us for a while. We just couldn't get rid of them. So whenever we saw them coming, we'd close everything up and pretend not to be home. Until one time, they showed up just when we were expecting company and had opened the gate. I said to them, 'Look, I don't have time to talk to you now, but why don't you come in for a drink? We've just opened a bottle.' That did it—they were gone in a flash, and they've never come back. I didn't even get a chance to point out to them that the good Lord didn't turn wine into water."

I laugh. But today, all this joking annoys me a bit. I feel Libby and Richard are making light of my problem. I am as relieved as they are that the question of their well can be dropped. But the fact remains that we don't know what happened. And I can't forget Libby's reaction when I told her of Renato's accusation. Strangely I sensed that her anger could just as easily have been directed at me.

It makes me realize that perhaps our friendship is not quite the same as before. They sit up here in their little castle, I think to myself, laughing at everyone. I was always attracted by their way of viewing the world in a comic light; I used to feel flattered to be included. But even in the old days, in some small corner of my mind I wondered if, as soon as I turned my back, they would be laughing at me, too.

"You should pay Renato a little social visit. To keep up good relations, *buoni rapporti*. Have you thanked him yet at all?" Libby looks at me in a motherly way. "These things are very important, you know."

The irises I picked are transforming themselves. The shriveled blossoms are beautifully black. Before they dry up and turn crisp, they get very wet, dripping with a dark purple fluid. It runs over my fingers when I pluck one off and splashes onto the marble dresser-top. At the same time, new blossoms are opening up. I notice a small leaf growing out of the stem like a shark's fin.

My life has fallen into a natural rhythm. In the mornings I work, drinking coffee, sitting at my table looking over at La Croce. It was hard to begin, but now I am back inside my ideas from eight years ago, as if no time had passed. They are good ideas, but my difficulty in arranging them has not gone away.

As I work, I hear the stirrings of life over at La Croce. A cock crows. Silvana yells at Sama, the hideous little dog they have just acquired, to "come here." Sama is barking because Andrea, the mailman, has arrived on his motor scooter. Silvana's voice as she greets Andrea carries clearly over to me. It's a deep, sharp voice, almost like a man's.

I let myself be distracted by any occurrence over there, however small. A figure walks across the space between the houses, and I pick up my binoculars to see who it is. Usually I can recognize the people with my naked eye, but I like to bring them closer. I observe the meeting between Silvana and Andrea, their gestures, Sama bouncing around. Someone, probably Flavio, goes into the shed below the big house and comes out again after a while carrying a bucket. Then he starts working on the field below the shed.

The distance makes these goings-on enigmatic. I feel as though I were reading words and sentences in a language I don't know.

Sometimes I see Flavio's father Elio, or the thin, bowed figure of his mother, Paola.

In the past I used to train my binoculars on Amedeo, the painter, standing in the field where Flavio is working now. Amedeo rarely seemed to do any work; more often he just stood there, leaning on his hoe. Once I saw him lift his shirt to readjust the large copper plate he wore over his stomach, for his liver, as he'd explained to us.

But even something as simple as a horse grazing near Riaccio, to the right of La Croce, or a herd of sheep no larger than grains of rice, entrances me. I strain to bring them into focus, to catch some rare and precious detail, like a jeweler examining a gem through his magnifying glass.

I pass my days mostly alone. In the afternoon I sit on the terrace, and unless I turn on my tiny short-wave radio, I hear no sounds except for the birds, the buzzing of insects, and occasionally a human voice far in the distance. If a car comes, I hear it long before it emerges from the woods; and like Richard, I stand and look, waiting to see who it will be. Fortunately, most of the cars turn and go in the direction of Castellina and Spazzavento. I don't want anyone to come up here. I don't want to see people or be seen. Solitude begets shyness. The house is my snail-shell.

Sometimes all the birds stop singing at once as if by agreement, and for a few seconds, I hear nothing.

In the evening after eating my supper outside I watch the sun, an orange ball, slide down toward the horizon, faster and faster. After it has gone, there is a period when the sky is still light and the colors in the landscape become more intense, almost glowing. As for the distant hills, it's hard to say what their color is; they seem transparent, like shadows.

And then I keep sitting there as the sky grows darker, the fireflies come out in the field below, and more and more stars emerge. You look at a spot, thinking it's empty, but if you keep looking they suddenly appear, whole patches of them.

An owl hoots up in the woods, close by. A thousand crickets make noise all around, and dogs bark down in the valley, responding to each other. And sometimes I'll hear the loud, raucous bark of the *caprioli*, the roebucks. It's a horrible noise, like choking on a fishbone. The first time I heard it I was frightened. Shadowy creatures spring away across the field.

A few times a week I go into town to buy groceries. I drive down to Vigliano and park in the little square. At the Co-op, I wave hello to Mario's son Marcello when I see him standing behind his butcher's counter. He waves back. He, too, is Silvana's nephew, Renato's cousin. I could stop and chat with him, but I don't. Perhaps it's his uniform: I feel a bit embarrassed for him. The meat counter employees are made to wear orange and green aprons—the orange part styled to look like a little vest—and white skipper's caps with mesh on the sides. I prefer to greet him out in the country, where he is his own man.

Marcello grew up at Casabassa. Now he lives with his mother, Franca, and his wife and children in the house down by the Villa where the Marchese moved them when he wanted to sell Casabassa. We used to pass by there frequently. Mario, Marcello's father, would come running when he saw our car. He would flag us down and invite us into the kitchen to share a *gocciolino* with him. After he died, we no longer went inside, but Franca would stop us if there was mail. In contrast to Mario's tipsy friendliness, Franca had an air of refinement and reserve. She would exchange a few distracted words of conversation, her voice trailing off vaguely as if her thoughts had already moved on to something else. The expression on her face could be described as veiled.

Marcello married a dark-skinned girl who couldn't have been eighteen. Emilia was very pretty, with big eyes and delicate features. They had two children, a boy and a girl. Marcello worked at first in the butcher's shop in the square and then, after a few years, at the Co-op. Emilia became transformed. She was no longer pretty. She had a gap in her teeth and a hardened look about her face. Libby told me that she had once seen her stumbling on the path, drunk. I saw her several times at the train station bar. But Marcello, who is only a few years older than me, hardly seems changed at all. He has red cheeks and a cheerful look. How can he be so cheerful? I wonder.

Because I have to conserve my money, I don't go to the little picturesque shops in the square that are favored by the other foreigners. I've even begun to buy some things at the new "Discount," where they sell goods straight from the cardboard boxes they were shipped in. It's not very picturesque, but I've seen nuns shop there, and nuns are picturesque. The young manager always looks gloomy, as if he were serving a long term in purgatory. One time when I enter the Discount, he is in the midst of shouting at an old man who is probably deaf: "A *vermicello* is just a thicker *spaghetto*!" He repeats this sentence several times with slight variations, as if relishing its absurdity. I have to smile. I come abreast of him—he is mopping the floor—still grinning. He doesn't look up until I am right in front of him, and then we both say *buongiorno* somewhat archly and ironically.

Years ago, before the Co-op or the Discount were built, there used to be a tiny shop on the road that carries on past the Fattoria Poggiogriffini to the village of Bibbiano. The proprietor of this shop, Enzo, catered to the foreigners moving into the area. He was not a Tuscan. He was a grotesquely fat man, unshaven and slovenly. He would cut himself a thick slab of his overpriced prosciutto and eat it between chunks of bread while leaving his customers to ferret in the dusty shelves for a can of tomatoes or a package of mealy cookies. When one had assembled some items on his counter, he'd put the remains of his sandwich down and begin to write bold yet totally illegible figures on his little pad, wheezing heavily while one waited in suspense.

He would interrupt his adding operation for a few words of conversation, which, because they came belatedly, seemed like a graciously bestowed favor. Enzo had the air of a man who knew what was really going on. His conversation was different from that of the peasants. He seemed like an intermediary between them and us, and between the Mugello and the larger world around it.

He had a wife, Adele, who was a little crazy. She wore flamboyant red dresses and Spanish combs in her long untidy hair. One day we came by the store, and boxes of her things were piled up in front. Distraught, she asked my parents if they could employ her "as an *au pair* in England." It turned out that Adele was not Enzo's wife after all, and on that day he was throwing her out. She invited us upstairs to her bedroom and showed us drawings that had been made of her when she was an artist's model in Paris. There could be no doubt: they were authentic sketches by well-known French painters.

Within a matter of weeks, Enzo made a trip to Rome and came back with a new wife. It baffled me how a man like Enzo could find a woman at all. This one, Carla, was the opposite of Adele: a solid fiftyish housewife, the kind you'd expect to keep her silver polished and her linens starched.

Unexpectedly one night, Enzo was found dead. He'd had a heart attack. Carla kept his shop going for a few years and then retired to a little house in Bibbiano, a few doors away from the old Marchese.

I still see Enzo's son sometimes. He is a bus driver in Florence.

12

On my first visit, I asked the Donatis: "How is Flavio? How are Elio and Paola?"

"*Bene*," Silvana and Costanzo both said, nodding expressionlessly. "*Bene*."

That's all they said. Although the distance between the doorways of the two houses is fifteen meters at most, there seems to be little traffic between them. The biggest house at La Croce is easily four times as large as the Donatis', but decayed and neglected. It holds a sinister fascination for me, like a haunted house. I wonder what it looks like inside. I imagine it as a rotted black honeycomb of empty rooms.

I've been in it only once. It was when Amedeo was still alive. He'd invited us to look at his paintings. We walked through a sort of parlor where all the windows were shuttered; in the gloom we could just make out two ancient crones sitting at a table, already absent from this world. Amedeo's paintings were piled up in a small room, dozens or perhaps hundreds of them. Battle scenes at sunset. Mad explosions of color: pink, purple, orange; canon fire rendered in thick streaks of red paint squeezed directly from the tube. Some of these now hang in the pizzeria in Vigliano.

Elio, though he is Costanzo's cousin, is made of a different material. My dislike of him goes back to an incident that happened many years ago. It was one of the rare occasions when my family joined the evening gathering at La Croce. We were the center of attention. Questions were addressed to us, but there was also a sense that the assembled group were explaining themselves to us, conscious of us as witnesses to their way of life. Marietta, the schoolteacher, lectured us on local history, while her brother Amedeo postured as a mad genius. At a certain point, Elio, feeling left out and wanting to have his part in the self-display, declared proudly that when he came home after a day of work he would throw one boot into one corner and the other into another—he illustrated this by kicking his legs out vigorously—and leave it to Paola, his wife, to pick them up and clean them off and set them side by side for the next morning. I remember being revolted by the stupidity of this boast, the only point of which seemed to be that Paola was his servant.

One day I run into Elio on my way to La Croce, and I have a chance to study his ignoble physiognomy up close. The drunkard's nose, shaped like a big drop of water, heavy and bulbous toward the bottom; the dim eyes. Whitish pustules in the pores of his skin. Thin, long strands of gray hair slicked back over his head with natural grease. And a little bit of unshaven beard under his chin, or perhaps this is simply what is left of his dwindling facial hair.

Not knowing what else to say to him, I comment on the weather. This drought, I say, repeating what I've been hearing, isn't very good for the crops. No, he agrees, shaking his head, not good at all. Then, gesturing up at the sky: *Faccia Lui*— "Let Him take care of it." "The Eternal Father will see to it." I've heard him strike this same note before, fake piousness seasoned with nasty sarcasm.

We always assumed that Flavio was mentally impaired in some way. Costanzo and Silvana were kind to him. Whenever he hung about their front door, making his cat and dog noises, they'd call his name, encouraging him to come inside. Costanzo used to tell us, smiling, "He's a bit strange." But over the years Flavio has gradually taken over most of the work on the fields that Elio neglected. I wonder now if perhaps his "strangeness" is not inborn, but the result of a childhood blighted by his horrible father.

I've begun visiting the Donatis more frequently in the evenings. After seeing no one all day long, it's good for me to have people to talk to. At first I worried that I was imposing on them. But one time, after I had kept to myself for several days, Silvana called me on the phone and asked reproachfully: "Why didn't you come last night? I baked a cake! Come tonight—Costanzo is always so happy to see you."

From the moment I approach their door, Sama, their new dog, starts up her ear-splitting barking. It's hard to see how this ugly animal can evoke affection. She has the face of a fox, a thick, bullet-like torso, and short legs that are airborne with each bark, the nails clicking as they come down again on the tile floor. Silvana's repeated admonishments— "Sama, be quiet!"—of course have no effect. There's something soulless, almost insect-like about the unabating frenzy. Yap! Yap! Yap! "Sama! Quiet!" A number of minutes pass in this way. Finally, Costanzo will carry Sama outside and close the door. Then they both look at me, chuckling as if the dog were a misbehaving child.

We talk about one thing and another, nothing much. The water doesn't have to be brought up anymore, and I don't upset my wine glass either.

Costanzo sometimes seems torn between our conversation and the program playing on the TV in the adjacent room. The sound is turned off, but his chair is positioned so that if he turns his head just a little, he

101

can see the screen. I can see it too if I lean slightly to the right, while Silvana has her back to it. Costanzo will note that a very important soccer game is being played between Italy and Germany, between the best teams of both countries. "The score is still 0-0." He hastens to add that he doesn't care about soccer. He doesn't care at all, he is not *sportivo*. The game, toward which his eyes keep sliding surreptitiously, doesn't interest him in the slightest—

"*Porca madoscaccia!*" He jumps out of his chair. "The Italians just missed scoring a goal!"

One evening we are chatting when the telephone rings. Silvana goes to the next room to answer it, and I sense once again Costanzo's alarm at being left alone with me. After listening for a moment, he informs me that it's a woman named Fiorenza who lives in Cetinale. She is telling Silvana about a wedding she attended in Florence. Costanzo pretends to be keenly interested in their conversation, closing his eyes in the effort to hear what is being said. Fiorenza is transmitting details about the wedding: the food, the number of people present, and the honeymoon destination, which will take the young couple twenty hours to reach. Every so often, Costanzo relays to me what Silvana is repeating, though I can hear it just as well myself. "Where are they going?" he prompts her several times, but we don't get an answer.

Silvana is out of my line of vision behind the door frame. As we listen to her, I look at the TV screen, where the show they were watching before I came is still silently going on. It's some sort of soap opera: well-dressed people move about in an opulent interior. I suddenly imagine that they are the ones looking at us through that glowing window, peering curiously into the Donatis' little house.

I've been inside that other room once or twice before. It's a small formal dining room, where the good plates and cups are displayed in a credenza and a large wedding portrait of Enrico and Armanda hangs on the wall.

"Twenty hours by airplane!" Silvana repeats with a big smile of incredulous amusement as she rejoins us. Where could they be going? Fiorenza wasn't sure herself.

"Who knows," Costanzo says with a grand sweep of his hand, buoyed with relief at Silvana's return, "maybe it's someplace near India."

"Or maybe near China," I contribute, in the same spirit. We all laugh and agree that we wouldn't want to do twenty hours *in apparecchio*.

"Not unless I could give myself a shot so that I wouldn't know anything." Costanzo vividly mimics the needle jabbing his arm; his head lolls.

"Did you two go on a honeymoon?"

My question causes Silvana to double over with hilarity. A honeymoon?! "Yes, for twenty minutes," she gasps.

Costanzo grins sheepishly. "Nooo, not twenty minutes."

But they did have a *festa*, a big lunch for all the relatives, and dancing afterward. They were married in the church in Bibbiano.

"Do you like to dance?" Silvana asks me. She doesn't seem very surprised when I say I don't know how, I've never danced.

"What about you?"

"Not now," Costanzo says with an embarrassed laugh. "Not anymore."

"But before?" I look at Silvana.

"Yes, before…" I've given her the cue she wanted. She starts telling me how from the time they were children, they were always dancing. They used to dance in the clearing made around the *carbonaia* while it was burning, or if they were sent to watch the animals, they'd dance in the pasture. "We danced all the time."

"Without music?"

"Oh, we'd sing the music. It was classical dance, of course, not the kind they do today: the waltz, the tango. The best was the tango," she adds firmly.

"Later, when we were older, in the summers we'd go down to Bibbiano to the big dance floor out in the open. And in the winter we'd organize dances at each other's houses, taking turns. We'd set out at night. They started at about ten. There were so many of us, and everyone knew everyone else. The girls could go only if one of their elder brothers came along. My brothers loved to go too, so it wasn't a problem. Except if for some reason both of them couldn't go at the same time; then there was nothing doing, no dance. I had to go to bed and that was that."

Her face falls at the memory of it. Her disappointment seems as keen today as it was fifty years ago. She describes how the dances carried on into the morning hours, there were so many people that the floors bounced, and late-comers had to be turned away.

"Because in those days, the houses were full of

young people. All the houses, even up in the woods, were inhabited. This whole area was full of people. In those days," she says, "we were happy."

I feel like poking a hole in this idyllic picture, which seems a bit too good to be true. "Wasn't there ever any trouble among the families," I venture, "with so many of them living close together?"

But Costanzo, who has been silent all the while, shakes his head. "There was brotherhood," he says decisively.

Another evening, I ask them if they remember the time of the war. I've heard that the Germans' last line of defense, the so-called Gothic line, ran right through this area.

"Yes, it's true," Costanzo says. "But the Germans retreated without firing a single shot. It was the others, the Allies, who were bombing and shelling left and right, just to make sure."

The peasants were all ordered to evacuate their farms and go to the other side of the valley, taking with them only what they could carry. Costanzo went to a different place from Silvana. Of course they weren't married yet then. Costanzo was just sixteen.

"We slept on the floor," Silvana says, "crammed side by side, thirty to a room, with at most a blanket underneath for cushioning. We were on the second floor of a house; the ground floor was occupied by German soldiers. One night a bomb fell into the room next to the one where we were sleeping. Everything was filled with smoke. We couldn't very well go down and join the Germans, so we climbed out the windows and slept in the chicken coop. We were away from home for forty-five days.

"And then there were the partisans and the Republicans, fighting each other. But they were *both* bad. I remember one day, my mother had just put bread in the oven, over at Casabassa where we were living, when two partisans came by with two Republicans whom they'd captured down by the Villa. They were bringing them up to the woods to shoot them. When they smelled the bread, they wanted some. They said they'd wait until it was done. So you see, the partisans were bad too, demanding food from us. If the Republicans had caught us giving it to them, they would have shot us all.

"Later, there were three of them coming back down from the woods. One of the Republicans switched sides and became a partisan."

We are all silent for a moment.

"One time," Costanzo says then, "my friends and I found a German who'd had the whole bottom of his face blown off."

Silvana: "Did he die?"

"*Porca miseria*, yes he died! We covered him with a blanket."

I usually avoid talking about the work I'm doing. But occasionally I feel I have to mention it, to avoid giving the impression that I merely spend my time "resting"—as Costanzo hypothesizes about Richard and Libby. This causes Silvana to reflect wistfully on how good it is for people to know things, to be educated and informed about the world. "Our life is just eating and sleeping and working. We haven't gone very far…"

Costanzo interrupts her impatiently, irritated by her expressions of inferiority and regret. "Yes, but in our time, when we were young, things were different. There were no school buses. We had to walk to school."

He only finished the fifth grade, Silvana the third. The elementary school was in Bibbiano; to go on to secondary school, they would have had to walk to

Vigliano, which takes an hour and a half.

"Costanzo was very good in school," Silvana says. "Writing, math, everything. The teacher even called his parents in to talk to them. She told them they should let him keep on with his schooling, he could go far. But there was no way he could go; he was needed at home."

I look at Costanzo, who nods briefly without raising his eyes, to confirm that this is true.

I feel ashamed of my easy life and the advantages I've had.

One evening as I approach the Donatis' house, I hear voices. I'd forgotten that it's Sunday, visiting day. Silvana has been urging me to come on a Sunday so that I can "see everybody." I know I should put in an appearance, but I've avoided it so far. Enrico and his wife Armanda will be there with their son Alvise, and perhaps some additional visitors. The idea of this crowd scares me.

But it's too late to turn back now. I may have been seen.

They've all just finished eating when I arrive. It's impossible to see how so many people can fit in the tiny kitchen, but everyone moves his chair an inch or so to make room for one more. Costanzo is standing by the sink, leaning on the kitchen table so as not to take up space.

I shake hands all around. Enrico and Armanda are both getting plump; Enrico is sporting a little brush mustache and a brightly patterned nylon shirt. Marietta is here, and her husband Salvatore, whom I never recognize from one time to the next—bottle-bottom glasses and gray beard stubble. Marietta is a tiny wiry woman who always seems to remember everything about me. As self-appointed cultural intermediary, she once recited for my benefit an entire poem, with many stanzas, describing some medieval battle that happened nearby.

She is already looking at me fiercely. Before she can get started, I turn to Enrico and ask how things are going with him.

He shrugs his shoulders: "Oh—we get by. One has to content oneself. No use complaining, right?"

He says it with a long-suffering air which suggests that he has much to complain and little to be content about.

Enrico works in one of the biggest factories in Florence, making lenses for military weaponry. A company bus brings workers from the Mugello to the factory and back every day. Silvana has told me that he has a position of authority. To all appearances, he and Armanda are doing quite well for themselves. They own an apartment in one of the nice new buildings near the Co-op in Vigliano, and they have just returned from a vacation in Paris. But Enrico always acts unfortunate, jealously wanting to hide what he has.

I feel uncomfortable around him and Armanda. The two of them are polite to me but not particularly friendly. Libby and Richard, who attend the meetings of the *comune* in Vigliano, say that Enrico distinguishes himself there by his anti-foreigner stance. "The foreigners have the houses. Let them pay for the roads. I have only a little piece of land and no house, so why should I have to contribute?"

His attitude is understandable. He sees the foreigners living well, apparently working very little, while his parents, who labored all their lives, barely scrape by.

Alvise, who was playing outside, comes in shouting: "The dog took it in the face!" He's been squirting the chickens and Sama with his big water gun. After being made to say *buonasera* to me, he starts begging Armanda for gum. She ignores him for a while, finally says to Enrico, "Hand me my purse." She says it twice, then gets up to reach for it herself. She unwraps a piece of gum for Alvise.

Marietta remarks: "I would never give a child a piece of gum. Gum is extremely dangerous for children." As Armanda ignores her, she repeats her point, fixing me with a critical stare. "It's true. In America, a little girl once choked on a piece of gum. Here it's called *gomma americana*."

I turn to Enrico again, trying to draw him out.

"How is your work going?"

"*Bene.*" He tells me that they are just finishing a big project of sighting systems for installation in the Czech Republic, and soon they will prepare a delivery for Syria. A few moments pass while I digest this information. Then I can't help asking: "Did you say, for Syria?" Enrico grins. "Yes, well, but for political reasons we aren't supposed to call it Syria but 'Finland Two.' We ship things to Finland, and from there they go on to Syria." He says it as if it were an open secret and a joke. Silvana smiles apologetically in my direction as if to say, "These subjects are above my head."

Then Salvatore starts asking me questions, how long I've been here and how long I'm planning to stay, and how many hours it takes by airplane to get here.

"And you?" I ask, before we can get to gas prices.

He responds with considerable liveliness. He and Marietta are going to move to Sardinia soon, for good. They have their own house there, a new house that they've been building gradually over the years. Everything is better in Sardinia than in Tuscany.

"What is better?" I want to know.

"Everything, everything." The whole quality of life. The food. The people. The weather. The cost of living. Everything costs less and is better. "We've finally decided to make the move, end of discussion. You can't breathe the air in Florence anymore, it's too polluted. It makes you sick. And here in the country, the former way of life is dead. The life of the peasants has become impossible in Tuscany. Whereas in Sardinia..."

I feel vaguely irritated by this talk and point out that Renato seems to be doing quite well. "And Lorenzo will carry on the farm after him."

As soon as these words are out of my mouth, I become aware of my insensitivity. Silvana and Costanzo are both silent.

Quickly changing the topic, I ask Salvatore about the trip to Sardinia, which he has said takes twelve hours by boat from Livorno.

"What's it like? Are there seats on the ship? What do you do for twelve hours?"

Salvatore laughs at my ignorance and starts describing the private cabins, beautifully appointed, with TVs and private baths, bowls of fruit and bottles of mineral water. The ship has everything, bars, TVs everywhere, a barber shop, even a swimming pool.

"It's like a whole village on the move!"

And on two floors beneath all of this, hundreds of cars are loaded up, buses, entire trains! He stands up to show how the first half of a train is loaded onto the ship and then the other half is put on the track alongside it.

Silvana and Costanzo listen, smiling, happy to marvel again at this description they've doubtless heard many times before. Silvana passes around her cake, but I am the only one who takes some; everyone else turns it down, saying they are too full.

At 10:30 I excuse myself and walk home.

13

I am sitting at my desk when I hear the sound of rain beating on the ground. But the sun is shining, there is no rain. I lean out the window to look. It's a herd of goats coming down the path. They are brown and white, young and old; the females have heavy udders and there is one shaggy white ram with a single large horn. They are eating the grass, the brambles, the flowers, munching everything in a businesslike fashion as they move on down the hill.

A little later there is a pounding on the front door as if someone were trying to break in. I go to the window again. There below is Klaus Ziegmann, getting ready to knock a second time with his walking stick.

Sensing my gaze upon him, he pauses, his walking stick in the air. His aging yet curiously boyish face turns up toward the open window opposite the one from which I am peering down. I quickly withdraw and run down the stairs to open the door before he has another chance at knocking a hole in it.

"I was walking by and saw your windows open," he says by way of introduction. "I am a neighbor of yours, Klaus Ziegmann. I am called

Claudio around here."

"I am very happy to meet you." I introduce myself as well, although the fact that he is speaking English instead of German shows that he knows perfectly well who I am.

I've heard a few things about him, too. The Ziegmanns came to the Mugello years ago together with another couple, their close friends. They bought the two adjacent houses below Renato's farm. The friendship ended when "Claudio" and "Sabina"—the other wife—started an affair. Their spouses left them and the two remained as neighbors, their short-lived romance replaced by an enduring and passionate hatred.

"Would you like to come in?"

"Oh no, no, absolutely not! I'm just taking my walk. I spend too much time indoors as it is."

He is taller than me, with reddish skin, blue eyes, and circular wire-rimmed glasses. The cherry-colored overalls conceal a slight paunch on his otherwise bony frame.

"I have to tell you that your shutters need repainting." He gestures toward the nearest one. "Look at this. They're in a terrible state. If you let them go like this, the wood will rot. And then you can just throw them away."

"Yes, I suppose you're right. I hadn't thought about it."

But this vague answer doesn't seem to satisfy him. "I've been noticing them for months," he persists. "They're fine shutters. It's a pity to see good workmanship ruined through neglect."

"I haven't been here very long. And to be honest, I've had more immediate worries. The water situation...."

"What is it that you do?" he asks. He doesn't seem aware of interrupting me.

"I'm trying to finish a dissertation in English literature. On Edmund Spenser."

"Ah!"

Silence.

"And what do you do?"

"I work! I work!"

The answer comes shot out in a tone of exasperation. I sense he's been asked this question before, in a skeptical way.

"I meant, what is your field?"

He scrutinizes me as if seeing me clearly for the first time. "My field is political philosophy."

"Oh!" I scan my brain for anything I might know about political philosophy, but come up empty. I try to look impressed.

Ziegmann looks at me more kindly. "Let me give you some advice," he says. "From one who has experience. Do not disagree with anyone in your dissertation. In fact, don't ever, *ever* disagree with anyone more powerful than you. On the contrary, you've got to learn to brush people's teeth. You know what I mean?"

I laugh, glad that his annoyance about the shutters has given way to a more jocular mood.

"Yes, brushing people's teeth, that's what I call it. You've got to go right *in* their mouth, brush *up* and down. I myself have not followed this advice. I have always insulted everyone to their face. Just a few months ago, I was at a conference in Memphis. Afterward, I wrote an article proving that everything people said there was bullshit."

He pronounces it *boolsheet*. I laugh again.

"When I was young, your age, a professor wanted me to change my doctoral thesis because I disagreed with him. But I was right, and he was wrong. What he said was all *boolsheet*. So I killed him later. But only in a footnote. He wasn't worth more than that."

Ziegmann is leaning casually on his walking stick as he speaks. Twice he nearly tips over as the stick slides off a stone. But he doesn't seem to notice.

"How long will you stay here?" he asks. He

must be anxious to regain his spot on the terrace.

"I was hoping to stay for some time. But I'm worried about the water situation. It's a bit mysterious. When I arrived, our cisterns were completely dry, and Wenzel said he hadn't had water all week. Now, at least, there's a little dribble coming in. But I'm afraid it could stop from one moment to the next."

"Ah—Wenzel! Better not mention my name to him."

"Why?"

"I think he doesn't like me."

I make a noise as if to say that couldn't possibly be true.

"Oh, I've given him reason not to like me. I told him off. Well, it's a long story."

Ziegmann switches to German, taking me into his confidence.

"You know that little building across from his house, that's totally ruined? When I first came here, you could have slept in it. The roof was caved in, yes. But it had walls, the floor was good. Now it is completely destroyed. I asked Wenzel one time why he didn't let Renato use it for his cows, and he started telling me off. And then *she* came out, acting like some Baltic lady-of-the-manor. So, I told them that the little building they had ruined was the *only* beautiful part of their property. And after that I wrote him a letter, telling him that morally he had no right to own the building in the first place, and he ought to give it to Renato, who could make good use of it. So you see," he concludes, "I think Wenzel probably doesn't like me now."

He looks very satisfied with the mortal blow he has dealt. I smile, but I feel for Wenzel as mentally I add Ziegmann to his long list of troubles. The Wenzels have probably drawn a line between what they can and can't handle. It's true that the side building has been allowed to decay, but the main house is looking better and better.

"Anyway," Ziegmann winds up, "if you're staying for a while, perhaps we can meet again. Perhaps I could be useful to you. Do you know Karl Popper?"

"I've heard of him."

The question implies that he knows the famous philosopher personally, perhaps as a friend; though I'm not even sure if he's living or dead. But no further explanation or offer of patronage follows. The name is left hanging in the air, vague as a threat.

Once again, I watch Ziegmann make his way down the rocky path.

He disappears behind Casabassa, but does not

emerge, as expected, on the road leading into the woods. Instead, a few minutes later I see him strolling with Renato, whom he must have met by the cow shed.

The philosopher in his red overalls, with his head bowed, his hands humbly clasped behind his back, is nodding sagely, actually listening, absorbing the wisdom of the peasant.

"Don't mind Claudio," Libby tells me. "He's all right. We avoid him ourselves. It's too bad, but what else can you do? He has a choleric disposition. It's his living situation. What a spectacle! He and Sabina are constantly calling the *vigili* on each other. One of them says the other is parking his car on their property, or making too much noise, or has hung their undergarments out to spoil the view. You can imagine the gossip they provide for the whole Fattoria. Alessandra takes care of both of their houses."

And she adds, "The poor man seems to be acquiring what we English call an expensive complexion. Though, of course, in Italy you can get an expensive complexion quite cheaply."

Ziegmann is right about the shutters. But they are not the only thing. I could easily allow myself to become obsessed about the disrepair into which Querceto is slowly but surely falling. Every morning when I go to my desk, there are three little fresh piles of sawdust on it. Sometimes I can see it drizzling down onto my paper. Woodworms. I find a ladder in the *stalla,* and I climb up and carefully seal the tiny holes with glue. But the worms must be everywhere, slowly eating away the great oak beams that hold up the roof.

Another person might get to work, fixing things—as my mother used to do, putting on an old work shirt and slaving away, happy at the thought that she was making some improvement. And look at the Wenzels. But I am lazy. Or rather, I think too much about it, I get all wrought up and by the time I calm down I am tired. Besides: where does the task end? Where does it begin? Should I knock down the nest that swallows have built into the outside wall, right at eye level, on the terrace? Every day I check up on the baby birds with their little round bald heads and their wide-open beaks shaped like those folded paper toys that schoolgirls make, that can be opened in two directions. Should I stuff up that hole, too?

A giant crack has appeared in the bedroom wall.

Perhaps the new cement roof that my parents had put on is too heavy, and is slowly pushing the house apart.

All of these things are meaningless if the house does not have water. Now it's coming in, but it could stop again. Not understanding what happened makes me uneasy. What kind of a situation is this, where it stops and starts, and there's no telling why? A tube leads from the stream to the spring. A storm in April broke the tube, or didn't break it. The Parkers, my friends, may be drawing our spring water out through their well. The Cavinis are doing their laundry; the Wenzels have their roses. And Renato's cattle must drink. Where does all this leave Querceto?

It occurs to me that I'm not thinking, as I should be, in terms of saying goodbye, but of holding on to the house, of saving it.

Do the Donatis know something more about the water than they are admitting? Probably. Renato is Silvana's nephew, so naturally their loyalty is to him.

I don't know—I don't much feel like thanking Renato.

14

The weather has become quite hot. The air is dry, and often toward evening a strong breeze comes up. The clothes that I hang up on the line dry in half an hour. Everyone is talking about the drought. There have been a few showers, afternoon thunderstorms, but not enough to make a difference. Costanzo says with a doom-filled voice that he has heard the climate is changing permanently.

But for me it is another splendid morning, the birds chirping, no action at La Croce. I sit at my desk with my milky coffee, my bread and jam, my writing things, binoculars, and I feel unaccountably happy.

I go shopping at the weekly market in Vigliano. I buy cheese, fruit, a cheap cup to replace the one I've broken. The town is full of people. The square is perfumed by flowers and the fragrance coming from the bakery. I see Richard and Libby emerging from the post office; I see the Sardinian shepherd whom I haven't encountered in years; and finally, strolling along, looking very dapper in freshly ironed blue jeans and a checked shirt, I see Renato. He looks startled to see me.

Back at Querceto, on my terrace, the lizards are

like miniature dinosaurs.

One evening I forget to close the upstairs windows before dusk, and some bats have flown in. They hang from the highest point of the rafters in my bedroom, their tiny upside-down bodies turning this way and that and their ears twitching as they pick up different sounds. They're too high for me to reach even with the broom. If I climb on a chair, they're gone in a second, swooping back and forth at lightning speed, everywhere but through the wide-open window. They are supposed to have sensitive hearing, so I try bombarding them with noise, with shrieks as high-pitched as I can make them. The bats hardly react. My screeching is probably like a whale's booming to them, inaudible, but I'm cracking myself up, breathless with laughter. After about an hour I've managed to chase them to another room, and there I open the windows and close the door and hope that they will be gone by the morning.

The Wenzels come and go. They appear so briefly down at Casabassa that by the time I become aware of their presence, they are already leaving again. They must come down from Stuttgart just for the weekend, an eight-hour drive if you're driving fast, which I imagine them doing, with steely determination. They arrive, they set their wicker chairs out onto the patio, but they rarely sit in them. They spend two days in frenetic activity, cleaning and constructing and painting. They nurse the rapidly growing hedge (though it can't keep out the flies from Renato's cow shed across the way) and train roses to climb the side of the house. And then the chairs are put away again, the shutters are closed and bolted with shiny new locks, the gate is fastened with the heavy chain, and the house is empty once more.

Frau Wenzel avoids me. Every time I pass by Casabassa, she quickly withdraws. Silvana remarks on this, too. "That woman, you never see her. When you pass by their house, immediately she disappears."

Unlike Silvana, I understand that antisocial impulse, her need for solitude. Our houses are too close together.

I meet up with Wenzel one Sunday not long after my expedition with Renato and Landi. He is wearing a big straw hat and going in and out of the workroom he has set up in his former *stalla*. There is a hum of machinery inside.

"Do you have water coming in again?" I ask him. I know that he must.

He bows with mock formality.

"Fantastic! What happened?"

I describe Renato's theories and Landi's manipulations of the tube.

"It all seemed very mysterious. I mean, how could he have been so sure it would come back after that? I can't help thinking he secretly went and opened some valve."

"As long as it's coming, there's no problem, right? I compliment you!"

And he turns to resume his work. I am puzzled and then exasperated by his attitude. I suppose it doesn't matter that much to him, after all. If the water comes, so much the better; if not, he'll just as soon buy it from Landi. As a cardiologist, he can probably afford it.

But when I see Wenzel raking his gravel in shorts and white socks and sandals, no different than if he were cleaning his already clean sidewalk in a thoroughly clean suburb of Stuttgart, I have to smile and can't stay resentful. It strikes me that he is at base an earnest, modest man.

Costanzo has gone back to work.

Silvana calls me in the late morning and asks if I want to come over and get some vegetables from her garden. We pick some early zucchini and lettuce, and then she invites me to come inside. A delicious aroma fills the kitchen. She must have put the cake in the oven just before I arrived. She turns the oven light on to take a look at it. "Not quite, it needs a few more minutes. We'll eat a little bit of it, even if it's still warm, right?" I say I like it best warm. "Shall we have some tea with it?" And she puts a nice fresh cloth on the table and brings out her elegant teacups and saucers and cuts a lemon. At her urgings I end up eating five slices; together we finish half the cake, albeit daintily.

"You'll go and tell Enrico and Armanda that I eat like a pig."

She seems hurt, as if I'd struck her. "Why do you speak to me like that?"

I hasten to reassure her that I was only joking.

Silvana finds it unnatural that the stores should carry all kinds of vegetables and fruits year-round. In the past, one used to have to wait for things to be in season. She has also heard on television that nowadays they make chickens in only sixty days—females in fifty, males in sixty days. Who has ever heard of such a thing? "It takes me five months to make a chicken!"

She keeps using this expression, "to make a

chicken," instead of "to raise a chicken," which strikes me as comical. "They feed it all kinds of stuff, and in the end, what is there?" With her hands she mimics a volume expanding, and—poof—a balloon bursting. "I need five months to make a chicken you can eat!"

She hears the sound of a car door slamming. It's Erbertino leaving. Erbertino is a cousin who has been helping Costanzo make a fence. She runs out to tell him to stop and wait a minute, then comes back and rummages in the pantry chest for a piece of newspaper she's saved. It's already crumpled and she flattens it out to wrap up a couple of eggs to give to Erbertino.

"Have I ever shown you the chapel?" she asks me when she comes back inside. The tiny building is between the Donatis' house and that of the Florentine couple, Domenico and his wife Francesca. I tell her I've never seen the chapel open.

"Come, I'll show you."

She unlocks the door and we step inside. There are two small wooden pews, fresh lilies and roses on the altar, and white candles bent over from the heat. She points out the "medieval" picture, a reproduction of a nineteenth-century painting of St. Francis, and the "handmade" plaster sculpture of the Madonna.

She tells me that when she was growing up, the whole month of May used to be dedicated to the Virgin

Mary. People from all the houses congregated every night for prayers in this chapel. I ask if there was a priest; she says no, the prayers were said by old women, either Costanzo's mother or Flavio's grandmother.

I remember those two old crones sitting in the big house.

Silvana calls everyone and everything "poor thing," including me. I'll say something to her and she'll agree with me: "You're right, *poverina*."

Or herself: "*Oioi*, I'm tired, *poverina*."

And I've discovered something else about her: her malice. It's an innocent sort of malice, a delight in maliciousness itself, a childlike love of giggling at other people.

One day I am driving down to Vigliano when I see an elderly woman holding out her thumb by the side of the road. It's such an unusual sight that I don't register at first what she wants; then I stop and back up to give her a ride. In the evening I tell the Donatis about my encounter. Silvana wants a description of the woman. She listens for a while with furrowed brow — nothing I say rings a bell — until finally her face lights up. "Ah! It was Irma! Now it's all clear. It must have been Irma! She was a smallish woman, wasn't she, who walks with a limp, like this"—she did an imitation—"and has tiny little eyes, *poverina*, that look sort of sickly..."

I have to shake my head: I hadn't noticed any of these unflattering details.

And of course now I feed the flame; I'm always trying to make Silvana laugh. I even recount the anecdote that Libby has told me about Brigitte Mandelbaum, who tried to earn money picking zucchini alongside the Albanians, and was fired because she didn't pick them fast enough.

The Mandelbaums live at La Roccia, the small house above Castellina. I've never met Gustav Mandelbaum, but I know his story, which is remarkable. He is an elderly man, a distinguished scholar of Indo-European linguistics who used to be a professor in Berlin. When the Nazis came to power, he lost his professorship; but he stayed in Berlin, assuming a common German name, and survived the Third Reich working as a taxi driver. When it was over, he had scraped together enough money to buy La Roccia. Brigitte is his second, much younger wife. A former businesswoman, she now takes lowly jobs in Vigliano.

Silvana is almost in tears from laughing so hard. "She was fired *per scarsa rendita*?" She gasps, clutching my arm as if to prevent herself from falling over, and succumbs to a new spasm. The very idea of a German sinking to such a level is hilarious—and then failing at it! It's too much.

I am sorry for having told this story the way I did.

One morning, I've just begun working at my desk when I hear unaccustomed sounds coming from the bottom of the hill, from the direction of Casabassa. Alarming sounds—first a very loud groaning, then a series of higher-pitched, anguished cries. Each cry is followed by a vibrant echo.

I listen with bated breath. The sequence is repeated. I've finally figured it out: one of Renato's cows must be giving birth in the shed across from Casabassa. The echo is made by the corrugated tin roof.

After the cries there comes a silence, during which I hear a dry hacking sound. Giorgi is cleaning out the water channels across the road with a hoe. I should feel grateful that he is performing this public service, but it's a hopeless project. It's so hopeless that I think it can't be a coincidence that he is doing it just now, not fifty meters from my open window. It's a hint that something needs to be done about the road. I'm sure Renato suggested it.

There it is again: the deep groaning, followed by screams. It's a terrible sound, an expression of pure pain that gives me a sympathetic sensation in the pit of my stomach. Probably the cow does not understand what is happening.

At eleven, when all is quiet, I walk down the hill. Lorenzo is there, too. He and Renato look exhausted but exultant, as if they themselves had produced the calf. Both the calf and its mother are inside the shed, out of view. Renato does not invite me to have a look. "It all went well," he says curtly.

"I wanted to thank you for fixing the water."

"You're welcome." Then he says: "Those channels need to be cleaned out. It's because they're clogged up and the water doesn't run off that the road is ruined."

Even at this moment, I can't let that stand. "They're filled up with dirt because of the tractors and trucks that come up and down the hill," I say flatly.

"Oh no, no, it's because of the water."

But he doesn't have a leg to stand on, since only

yesterday I saw him towing a lumber truck up the hill with his tractor. And it has hardly rained in weeks.

15

There is a path that leads from Querceto up into the woods. I've begun taking short walks after my morning's work. You walk a couple hundred meters in the direction of La Croce; then, instead of following the path curving to the right, you keep going straight up a steep rocky slope.

A little ways along, there is a road altar to the Madonna set into the rock wall. It always has a few fresh flowers in it. It commemorates a miracle that happened many years ago. A boy was riding on a donkey up in the woods. The animal took fright at something and bolted, throwing the boy off. But his foot was caught in the stirrup and he was dragged down the hill as the donkey ran, his head banging on the ground, his skin stripped off. Yet when the donkey finally came to a halt, miraculously, the boy was still alive. Silvana told me this awful story, to which I could find no response.

Soon after that you come to a house without a roof which belongs to a man from Vigliano. He can't afford to rebuild it, but he spends his weekends here and has planted himself a tidy little vegetable garden. Where does he get his water from? Does this ruined house have a well? A spring of its own?

Alongside the path runs a thick bundle of tubes carrying water from the several springs that belong to La Croce. I am envious of these tubes and of the large cement reservoirs collecting the water at intervals.

Once in the woods, the path becomes effortless, winding on with barely noticeable climbs and dips, dappled with sun. The trees are mostly chestnut, with some oak and pine mixed in. The ground feels springy and the scent of last year's pine needles rises up from it, alternating with other smells, of flowers, leaves, earth, each smell borne on its own little gust of warm air.

Now and then I am startled by a sudden loud rustling in the underbrush. But it's only a bird or a lizard moving through the dry leaves. As I walk on, with all my senses alert, I begin to feel as though I were on a stage: as though I myself were being watched with the same keenness with which I am registering my surroundings. I come to a place where a rivulet has made a chocolate-colored puddle in the path. Specks of light dance on the water, and on its edge a large black butterfly with a white rim lazily pumps its wings up and down. I feel like drawing someone's attention to it—whoever it is watching me.

Why is it that my family never explored the

woods behind Querceto? Perhaps the answer lies in this word, *behind*. Our gaze was always toward the panorama of the valley. We were so used to thinking of Querceto as surveying the landscape below that we forgot the mountain behind our back.

Each time I take a walk, I venture just a little bit further, pushing myself to overcome my fear. I tell myself that it's silly to be afraid. It's unlikely I will encounter anyone; although you never know, there may be wood-cutters, or mushroom-seekers. But it's a more basic fear that I feel, of the unknown, of the silence, of being all alone in the woods.

To be honest, there is also the thought of Flavio at the back of my mind. I've seen him a couple of times recently, but only from a distance. Once I mistook him for Enrico as he came driving past in his car; I waved enthusiastically before realizing my error. When I saw who it was and how weirdly he grinned back at me, I was alarmed. I am worried by the thought of the frustrated sexuality in a mentally disturbed young man.

On one of my walks I find a clearing, and there is a tiny hut. Like the sheds at La Croce, it is made of old billboards; its walls are decorated with printed letters, some right side up, some upside down. There is even half of a green Bologna/Roma *autostrada* sign. I feel a surge of excitement. This must be the cabin that Costanzo and Silvana use in the fall when they gather chestnuts. Silvana has mentioned it often. It's all closed up. I try to peer through a crack, but it's too dark to see anything inside.

On my way back I find wild strawberries by the side of the path.

I am about to call *Permesso* at the Donatis' doorway when I see Silvana down to my left, behind the fence of Maia and Manfredo's garden, spraying water from a hose.

"I'll be right up," she calls when I wave to her. "Go on in. Costanzo's inside. I'll be right there." And she begins calling, "Costanzo! Costanzo!" so that he will come to the door and usher me in.

But I walk toward her. The sight of her there is somehow unusual and charming. She has her cardigan thrown over her shoulders and is standing motionless in the shadow, the arching spray from the hose white against the darker evening sky. She looks vulnerable. I can suddenly imagine her as a young girl.

"Can I come and look?" I ask, as I hesitantly approach. And she seems happy at this unexpected turn, this departure from our visiting routine. She shows me the Germans' garden, grumbles frankly about being expected to water it. "I have my own work to do." But they are arriving tomorrow. She points out to me the radar dish on top of the little converted school building. "With this," she says, "Manfredo can send lessons back to his students in Germany. Without telephone wires! Claudio has one too. This way, they can spend six months at a time in the Mugello, teach their classes without going back." I share her astonishment at this technological miracle. Silvana is suddenly overtaken by a fit of giggling. "All that," she says, looking at me, overcome with mirth, "all that, while we here, all we can do is make some macaroni, some cakes..."

Later, in the kitchen, I tell them about my walk, how I followed the tubes and came to their cabin.

"Then you were walking in my chestnut grove!" Silvana exclaims, *nella mia marroneta*, with a sentimental smile as though I'd seen something intimately hers, but that she is happy to share.

"If you'd gone a little farther, you would have come to a house," Costanzo says.

"I'm a little afraid of walking in the woods by myself."

"Nooo." A grin cracks on Costanzo's face.

"Afraid? There's nothing to be afraid of!"

Silvana laughs outright. "Afraid! There's nothing to be afraid of around here, you know."

"But how can there be a house higher up in the woods?" I ask. "How could people live up there?"

"Not anymore," Silvana says. "But before, in the old days, they lived up there all right. They had fields, they kept animals. They traveled to the village on horses or mules."

"The house is called Il Castagnolo," Costanzo informs me. Little Chestnut Tree.

And there were houses even higher up than that, they tell me, farther away, hidden still deeper in the woods.

"Back then," Costanzo says, "the winters were terrible. When it snowed, it really snowed, not like nowadays. You could get a meter, even a meter and a half, in one night. They could be cut off from the world up there for months at a time. With no electric light, and it gets dark early in the winter. Of course, no telephone, no doctors. Women gave birth, people died."

"But in the summer," Silvana quickly adds, "in the summer it was all right. The young people would come down from the woods to go dancing in Bibbiano. There were those two beautiful girls—"

"One winter," Costanzo says, continuing his train of thought, "a terrible *disgrazia* happened. A man had gone to visit another family, and in the afternoon it started to snow. In the evening when he wanted to leave they told him, 'Don't go, spend the night with us.' But he wanted to go by all means, thinking that his family would worry. He knew the path so well. Along the way he fell into a snowdrift and couldn't get himself out. It was several days before search parties could set out from Vigliano to look for him. He was completely frozen."

After Costanzo has told this story, we are all silent for a few moments.

"I myself," he says then somberly, as if speaking of a dusty historical exhibit in the *Museo Comunale,* "had an aunt who grew up in the woods."

I've made the acquaintance of two little girls, Elsa and Viola. They came walking over from La Croce with two tiny black dogs on leashes, peering curiously all around. One of them looked in the window and when I waved at her, she ran away in fright. Moments later, there was a pounding at the front door. There they stood with their little dogs.

"Is the little girl with red hair here?"

"No. What's her name?"

They look at each other. They don't know.

"She doesn't live here."

They stare at me in disbelief.

"If I see her, I'll tell her that you came looking for her."

They must be connected to the Florentines, Domenico and Francesca, who seem like nice people; we greet each other in passing. As the girls keep standing there, one of the little dogs runs past me into the house. I don't even notice it at first, I am busy trying to understand what they are murmuring to each other about a "*casa*." Perhaps they've just realized they've come to the wrong house. Then the girl whose name is Elsa says, pointing behind me, "My dog has gone into your house. May I come in?" I realize that this accident happened on purpose. She takes her time looking all around, then politely comes out again with her pet on the leash.

If I thought that, having failed to find their red-haired friend, they would leave, I was wrong. They sit down on the log next to the front door and we chat. They have a very grown-up way of speaking.

We hear a voice shouting in the distance, Domenico calling them from La Croce. "We're here!"

Viola yells back defiantly, as if to say, "and we're not coming back!" Domenico shouts again, and they deliberate for a moment what he is saying. "Our uncle said he's doing the cherries now." But they ignore him, they are more interested in talking to me than in picking cherries.

"Do you have a cherry tree over there? How lucky you are!" I tell them about how we planted some fruit trees, but the Marchese's goats ate all the leaves and so they died. Finally I say, "Well, I have to go back inside now."

They just look at me. I step over the threshold. "Bye, see you later."

They stand up and smile. "Bye, we'll come back again in a little while. At least we can chat a little more out here." They skip away with their little dogs.

I haven't seen them again. Perhaps they were visiting from a distant city.

16

Lorenzo has come to harvest the hay from our field. He simply shows up one morning. I am working at my desk and I hear the sound of the tractor coming up the hill.

I get up and watch as he turns into our field and begins slowly making his rounds, cutting the beautiful tall grass. I stand by the window where he can't see me.

I go back to my desk. Then I get up again to watch him. I wish I could go out and talk to him.

After a few minutes, I have to laugh out loud. The contrast between us is too extreme. Here am I, shut inside the house, all wound up from the effort of writing a few paragraphs, while he, out there in the open, drives placidly round and round the field on his tractor.

I find it strange that someone younger than I should have so much patience. What does he think about as he mows one field after the other, day after day? Renato owns fields all over the area, down in Bibbiano as well as out past Cetinale. Is Lorenzo's mind peaceful, Buddha-like, filled only with the task at hand?

The tractor is truly enormous. He sits up high

on it, looking down at everything. I wonder if it gives him a feeling of power. I suspect that Renato lets him drive the biggest machinery as an inducement, to keep him on the farm.

At noon he'll go home to a lunch cooked by Alessandra, then they all have a nap. Then he goes back to the field, then supper, sleep, and the whole thing starts again the next day. On weekend nights he'll go dancing.

He seems nice. I've heard that he has a *fidanzata* who is a hairdresser in Borgo. I wonder what she looks like. Does she want to live on a farm? Does he worry about that?

In the afternoon he returns with an implement attached to his tractor that stirs the hay up and turns it over so that it will dry evenly. Again I stand and watch him from the window. When he passes by the front of the house on his way home, sitting so high on his tractor that he can look straight into the second-floor windows, I retreat to one of the back rooms.

Libby told me that Lorenzo's dog, the German shepherd that used to go everywhere with him, was "gored by a pig," and Lorenzo didn't eat for three days. Richard corrected her, saying the dog wasn't gored by the pig; rather, the pig attacked it and chased it into the path of a car. It was killed instantly. Lorenzo used to carry the dog on his moped, its paws resting on the handlebars between his hands, when he went riding up in the hills.

Within a few days, the cut hay has turned pale. Lorenzo comes with yet another attachment, sweeping it into neat lines. The following morning he returns with the machine that rolls it up into big cylindrical bales. Every time the machine is full, it honks. Then Lorenzo switches something, the sound of the motor goes down, and another bale is released.

In the evening after he is gone, the giant *rulli*— several days' work—lie in a random configuration as if carelessly scattered on the field.

I feel it is a bad sign that Lorenzo came to take the hay from our field without so much as a nod having been made in my direction. It seems like a snub, or a provocation. Maybe Libby was right about paying Renato a social visit. The business with the water has made it clear that I can't afford not to be on friendly terms with him.

I've decided to go around noon, pretending that I'm just taking a stroll like Ziegmann, stopping by on the spur of the moment. To go in the evening seems too formal; it would be giving myself, as "a woman alone," too much importance. Besides, it's a long way to walk in the dark.

I realize my mistake as soon as I reach Renato's farm. Some builders are working on a scaffold on the side of the house; they stare at me curiously. It's the middle of the day: people are busy. This is no time for a visit. Renato is just crossing the yard. He looks unpleasantly surprised at the sight of me. His face clearly asks, "What do you want?"

"I just came by to say hello." Even I can hear how ridiculous this sounds. Renato looks incredulous for a moment. Then he waves his hand toward the front door.

"Go up and see Alessandra. She's inside."

I climb the narrow staircase. Alessandra is in the middle of cooking lunch. A large bowl of browned meat stands on the table; she is frying onions, herbs, and garlic. It seems she is going to feed the masons as well as her family.

"You came to say hello?" Alessandra continues stirring the pan. She looks still prettier than I remembered her. She seems to have had her hair done professionally, and there is no longer any gold in her teeth. Many people on the estate, including Costanzo and Silvana, have acquired dentures since my last visit.

I wish I hadn't come. The whole idea was misbegotten. But I can't simply turn around and go back down the stairs. I ask Alessandra about the renovations they are making to their house. She responds vaguely. I steal a glance around the kitchen, which is vast compared to the Donatis'. Some preserved animals, an owl and a ferret, are displayed on a high shelf. A poster-size baby photo of Lorenzo with a pacifier against a sky-blue background hangs on the wall.

"So, your *fidanzato* didn't come this year?"

I feel myself flush. Her question seems brutal, as if she were saying, "Enough niceties. Tell me something real."

The last time I was here with my *"fidanzato,"* he insisted on renting a sporty red car. He drove it ruthlessly on the unpaved roads, leaving behind clouds of white dust and angry faces. It's the image of that car that comes to my mind now.

"We're not together anymore."

Alessandra gives me a quick look. The gentle sizzling of the onions and the mixed fragrances of herbs and meat create a warm pocket of silence around us.

"I don't think we were right for each other."

"He wasn't good enough for you."

I realize with amazement that she has given the matter some thought. I feel a surge of gratitude that almost brings tears to my eyes. The Donatis' silence on the subject was tactful, but I interpreted it as disapproval. Having known each other since childhood, they probably can't understand the concept of a relationship that doesn't succeed.

Alessandra puts down her wooden spoon and turns off the burner. "Come on," she says brusquely. "I'll show you the renovations."

We go to see the new shiny bathrooms, and the bedrooms, theirs and the one that will be used by Lorenzo and his wife after they marry. There are parquet floors instead of the usual terracotta tiles, "because wood is warmer in the winter." New doors of solid cherrywood.

"It's costing us a sack of money," Alessandra says several times. I know this is a reciprocal confidence and I am supposed to ask how much, but I can't bring myself to ask. I praise the quality of the faucets, the beveled mirrors, feeling embarrassed by these details.

"I should let you get back to your cooking."

"Wait, I'll give you your phone books." Alessandra bends down to retrieve a bulky parcel from the bottom of a cabinet. "The phone company dropped them off with us a few months ago because they didn't want to go any further on the road. We've been keeping them for you."

When I come out of the house, Renato nods approvingly.

"Ah, good, you picked up your phone books!"

His manner seems more friendly now, as if, given this pretext, my visit hadn't been a faux pas after all.

17

Silvana has explained the way to me.

"There's a flat stretch, with big chestnut trees on the left, and then after the bend in the road you'll see the little path that goes steeply up. You can't miss it." She beamed, picturing it, *la mia marroneta.* "After the stream, keep to the left, always to the left. Otherwise, you'll end up in the ditch."

I'm setting out to find Il Castagnolo. Silvana has assured me that there is a path coming back down on the other side, past Castellina.

I pass the roadside Madonna, the house without a roof, and the turn-off that leads to the Donatis' cabin. I follow her instructions; it all seems perfectly straightforward. But after I've walked for about twenty minutes on "the path that goes steeply up," it suddenly ends. Or perhaps it ended a while ago, or I took a wrong turn somewhere. Though it seemed like a path as I was going forward, it looks like nothing at all when I look back. No path. The track I've been walking on is only a natural ridge along the side of the hill.

I try retracing my steps. Then I glimpse a streak of white higher up. I reach it by scrambling through the brush, battling aside thorny branches. Here is a nice, broad path. But as I follow it, it begins to slope downhill, imperceptibly at first and then inexorably, until I am near the bottom of a gully cut by a small mountain stream, much like the one I visited with Renato and Landi. This must be "the ditch." There is nothing for it but to go back up.

I spend another half hour trying in vain to find any of the landmarks that Silvana mentioned. It's no good. I am lost. I'm not sure whether or not I ought to be afraid. I sit down on a fallen tree bough and eat the food I have with me, an apple and some chocolate, as if anticipating the pangs of starvation.

I tell myself that this isn't exactly a jungle.

There are basically two directions, up and down, and either way I will eventually come to a point from which it will be easier to get my bearings. I decide to go uphill, not bothering about a path, and continue until I get to the top.

As I climb through the scrub on thick layers of brown leaves, I find mysterious yet reassuring remnants of civilization: a little piece of stone wall and, later, a short stretch of barbed wire fence. What purpose could these possibly have served, here in the middle of the woods? The trees start to thin. More and more sunlight is coming through. And then suddenly there is a clearing—and there is the house. It stands before me in the open sun, surrounded by tall grass. I stand gazing at it, breathless. I realize only now that I've been practically running. There isn't much left of its roof, and I can't tell for sure where the front door would have been. Small trees are growing in its rooms and one wall is entirely engulfed by brambles.

I take a couple of steps toward it. A small herd of *caprioli* spring off, startling me, making their unearthly noise. I've never seen them from so close before. They are tiny deer, lithe and graceful.

I walk all around the house. At the back there is a spring with a stone basin fitted around it. The *caprioli* must come to drink here. And from here I see a broad, unmistakable path about a hundred meters below the house, big enough for a car. That must be the path I was meant to find.

I drink some water and rest for half an hour, reclining against a piece of wall in the sun. There are wildflowers all around me, bumble bees and birds. It's so peaceful, I don't want to leave. I have to force myself to get up and begin my descent homeward.

I've been walking for about ten minutes when I hear the moped. It's coming from behind, and I have a confused thought of finding a place to hide by the side of the road. But it's already too late: it's slowing to a stop. I turn around. It's Flavio.

"*Ciao,*" he says. He has deep circles around his eyes.

"*Ciao,* Flavio. How are you?"

"*Bene.* And you?"

It's the first time I've seen him up close. He is definitely unwashed. He is my age or even a year or two younger, but the skin around the edges of his face already looks hardened and withered.

"I'm staying at Querceto for a while," I say, as casually as possible.

He nods and grins: this is old news.

"I was just taking a walk. I found the house up there..."

"You found the house!" Flavio seems to think this is funny. He laughs a machine-gun laugh, pointing his finger at me as if to say, "You're a good one!"

"And you? Are you going for a ride on your *motorino*?" I find myself speaking as if to a child.

Flavio mumbles something about *funghi.* He takes a plastic bag out of his pannier and holds it open for me to see. It contains five large porcini mushrooms. They are perfect specimens. They'll fetch a good price if he sells them.

"How beautiful! You must know all the right places!"

Again he nods, grinning. He returns the bag to

the pannier and revs up his motor again.

"*Ciao!*" He gives a wave and is off down the hill, in a cloud of dust and small stones and the racket of an old machine.

Relief floods through me as I resume my walk down the looping path.

It turns out that the house I found was not Il Castagnolo, but another one higher up.

"So you got lost, up there in the woods?" Costanzo looks at me with quiet amusement.

I tell them about my encounter with Flavio.

"*Poverino,*" Silvana says. "Poor thing, he's very unhappy. Soon he has to start working for ANAS, on the highways."

"It's just work," Costanzo interjects. "And he's not unhappy. It's the work I do, and Elio did."

"*Poverino,*" Silvana says again, looking at me. "He wants to stay up here. He wants to be on the fields, in the woods. I understand him. He's like me, he doesn't want to leave."

"Oh, be quiet. Bring her something to drink."

I agree with Silvana. I feel sorry for Flavio. I imagine it will be horrible for him to go to work for

ANAS. He will have trouble being accepted by the rest of the crew. They may not be kind to him because of his strangeness. But his family needs the money to live.

I go to pick up my mail at La Croce around noon, and Silvana walks back part of the way with me because she wants to go up into the woods. A few days ago there was a bit of rain, and she wants to see if there are any mushrooms. As we reach the bend in the road we hear a car from the direction of Querceto. Silvana stands still to see who it is. Recognizing Marcello, she quickly kisses me goodbye on both cheeks. She doesn't usually do this; it seems a bit strange. Perhaps she's trying to get rid of me so she can chat alone with Marcello. I don't take the hint but stand waiting for him along with her, glad for this chance to make up for any neglected friendliness in the Co-op. He is blushing and tongue-tied; he has a sandwich wrapped in blue plastic on his dashboard. He, too, is on his way to look for mushrooms during his lunch hour. The Co-op doesn't re-open until five o'clock.

I ask about his family, mentioning Emilia by name but not his mother, even though I know Franca better. I don't know what impulse made me do this:

perhaps an obscure desire to show respect to his wife just because she doesn't necessarily deserve it. I imagine not many people ask about her.

"*I bambini?*" I say, unsure how many there are now. It turns out he already has grandchildren. Although we are only a few years apart, the generation gap between us is continually widening. He seems in a hurry to get up the mountain. He is so shy and rosy and innocent-seeming. But he has an unpleasant, high-pitched giggle which makes me feel there is another side to him.

I think to myself how different the three cousins are: Renato, Enrico, and Marcello, the butcher.

I run into Enrico now and then in Vigliano, too. Seeing him is like a cold shower. When we were both younger we used to be on quite friendly terms; now when we talk there is a noticeable strain. It's clear he doesn't like my friendship with his parents. To him it must seem unnatural, contrived, a pretense. He must think they are taken in by it because they have no concept of my life in America. From his perspective, my familiarity with them could not be anything but condescending.

I think of Costanzo, working out his last months on the highways. It's true that he has changed, and it's not just the illness. He'll reach for the wine bottle a second and a third time, with a sullen, obstinate expression. Silvana gives him a look. It's not like him. It's as if he were saying, "Why should I behave any differently than Elio? We're the same, aren't we?"

Poor Costanzo. He sits there in his yellowed undershirt, bare-shouldered, strong and muscular yet at the same time also weak. What does he have to show for his life? Looking over at Renato's prosperous farm, he must feel cheated. I remember how he said, of the old days, "there was brotherhood." *Fraternità*—such an old-fashioned word. I understand what he meant now. While Silvana is nostalgic for the happiness of their youth, Costanzo looks back to a time when the peasants were all equal, when there were no distinctions between them. Since those days, the differences have grown wider and wider, like paths that started in the same place, some going to the top of the hill and others into the ditch.

Even the foreigners validate Renato's success. They are attracted to it like moths to the lamplight. They all flock to his loggia in the evenings. Everyone is welcome, Flavio too. It's a *festa* every night, and what's wrong with that? While in the Donatis' humble little kitchen, in the silences between utterances you can hear the single log crackling on the fire, the precarious pyramid of dishes drying on the cloth on the table.

Costanzo is too intelligent not to see how it all happened, how a thousand different reasons, of luck, circumstance, and character, each one by itself so slight and mutable, became fused together by a terrible logic into something made of iron, surprisingly simple in shape. It was his fate.

18

The summer is going by. The grass and brambles have grown high around the house again. After seeing Costanzo struggle with the machine the last time, I refuse to let him cut it anymore. Silvana keeps saying Enrico will do it. But there's no reason I can't do it myself.

I remember that we used to have a big scythe, a beautiful old thing with a hand-beaten blade. I look for it everywhere. I can't find it.

Then I vaguely remember we lent it to Costanzo several years ago and never got it back. Costanzo said something about needing to fix it.

I head over to La Croce to ask for it. But Silvana says, "Oh, that was broken, the handle came out long ago because it was dried out by the sun. I don't even know where it is now."

And now a suspicion comes to my mind. If the handle had come out, wouldn't they have simply taken a piece of wood and made a new one to fit? Perhaps they sold it. These old agricultural implements are collectible as antiques. I've heard that dealers come out into the countryside looking for just such things. And the peasants are only too glad to get rid of them and

160

buy new, machine-made tools.

But there's nothing I can do about it.

"Use my sickle," Silvana says. "Come on, we'll go find it. I left it in the vegetable garden." Sama, hopping and yelping and nipping at my heels, comes with us.

"Sama! Stop it! Don't mind her, she won't do anything. Sama! *Porco pinco!*" She giggles at her own swearing.

We pass by the rabbit cages; the chickens are wandering about freely in the fenced yard. Sama's excitement gets on a rooster's nerves and it lunges at her, sending her scampering to Silvana's side in fright. Silvana has put an old yellow kerchief on top of her head without tying it, as protection from the sun. The bib of her apron is pinned to her dress, a safety pin in each corner; perhaps the strap was torn.

She darts about among her rows of squash and cucumbers, looking for the sickle.

"Where did I put it? I was just using it this morning! *Oioi*, how stupid I am! But where is it?"

She is trampling heedlessly on lettuce heads, and there is a little piece of wilted lettuce stuck to the back of her cardigan. I notice her thin calves, encased in heavy stockings, all muscle and sinew, like the legs of certain animals which seem so frail yet possess

161

tremendous strength.

Finally she finds the sickle leaning against a water barrel, in the very place where it should have been all along.

It is almost completely useless. I work for two hours, hacking away at the brambles, grabbing tufts of grass with my left hand while swinging at them with the sickle in my right. I am exhausted, drenched in sweat, yet in the end I have cleared only a narrow strip. It looks ragged and ugly.

Going to return the sickle to Silvana, I've just passed the bend in the road when I see a dog on the path. Not Sama—a big dog. I've been walking with my head down, lost in thought; now I look up and see more dogs, three or four, big shaggy white and black ones like the ones down at Riaccio.

I do what I always do in such a situation. Without hesitation, I turn in my tracks and start walking back in the direction of Querceto, at the same casual pace, hoping the dogs won't get the idea that I've changed my mind because of them.

Then I hear Silvana call my name. I turn around. She is standing at the end of the path next to a man I don't recognize.

"Are you afraid of the dogs?" she calls out.

"Yes!"

"Don't be afraid! Their master is with them. They won't do anything to you!" Obediently I begin to advance again in their direction, though slowly and even exaggerating my fearfulness so that the owner won't let the dogs come too near me.

Finally I meet the famous Lodovico. I've seen the woman several times in passing Riaccio, bedraggled-looking, with long hair. Lodovico is old and weathered, but fairly tall and with a strong and upright body. He is wearing some kind of filthy sweater and trousers. He has a large head and only a single tooth in the upper left side of his mouth, covered in silver. He does not greet me or introduce himself, but immediately starts telling me how I ought to behave with dogs.

"You have to stand still, then all they'll do is come up and sniff you. Even a dog that bites won't bite you as long as you're standing still. But if you turn around and move away, you're inviting them to follow. Then even a friendly dog might bite you."

I resent this sort of lecture. I reply that I can't help my reaction, it's natural to be afraid of a dog you don't know. "I am a creature of instincts, too."

He repeats his truisms once more, then goes back to talking to Silvana. Despite his one tooth, he has a beautiful and clear way of speaking.

They are talking about his hands; he's saying he can't afford to go to a specialist. I look at them and am horrified. They look like hand-shaped balloons over-filled with air. Silvana asks about his leg, and he pulls up his trouser to show that that, at least, is better. Still a bit swollen, perhaps, but it doesn't hurt. Whereas his hands hurt so much that he can scarcely do anything with them, all the way up to his forearms.

As he points, I notice he is missing the little finger of his right hand. Perhaps it was bitten off by one of his dogs, I think to myself maliciously.

"I used to cut bread for the whole house, and now—nothing."

I ask what the problem is.

"Pains," he says. I just look at him. "Maybe arteriosclerosis," he relents.

He says goodbye to Silvana, and we watch as he heads toward Querceto, preceded by his dogs. He leaves the path and cuts across the hillside, where he begins calling out some incomprehensible gibberish in an altered, high voice, chanting commands to his dogs which are now chasing a large herd of goats across the field.

"Look how many goats," Silvana says.

I think of the sheep, the pigs.

"I've just come to return your sickle," I say, handing it to her. I can tell she was working in her garden, so I say goodbye and start walking back toward Querceto. But I can still hear Lodovico and his dogs nearby, and I turn around several times to look at Silvana for reassurance. After telling me repeatedly not to be afraid, she finally says, "I'll come with you."

Laughing at me the whole way, she walks with me as far as the bend in the road, giving me a finger to hold, as if I were a little girl and not thirty-five years old.

I ask Costanzo and Silvana about the price of doctors, because I heard Lodovico saying he can't afford to go to one, and I thought medical care in Italy was free. The answer is that visits to the family physician in Vigliano are free, but if he writes out a referral to a specialist, then it's impossible to get an appointment in less than three or four months unless you go to a private doctor.

"Take Armanda's father, who died last March. They had just celebrated Alvise's birthday. A few days later he felt unwell. He thought perhaps it was because he'd worked too hard the day before on the house he was helping his son build—that he'd broken a sweat, caught a touch of influenza. Instead of going to work the next morning, he decided to see the doctor, who ordered an ultrasound. He had to go to a private specialist because the public one could give him an appointment only after six weeks. Well, of course, by that time he was dead and in the ground. The private doctor found that he was all full of tumors inside. There was nothing they could do. He was seventy, but still youthful, very strong."

Silvana is telling me all this. "The next Sunday, the family were eating together again. He knew, and his family knew, how things stood with him, and yet he talked and ate just the same as ever. He helped himself to ravioli three times. Three times!"

Her tone is the same as if she were saying, "Three tears appeared on the face of the Virgin." That last defiant act, sending all those ravioli down into the stomach filled with tumors, was like a kind of miracle.

Costanzo looks uncomfortable. At one point, his tongue is sticking out of his mouth as he glances sideways at Silvana, giving him an almost cretinous aspect. It's not hard to guess the direction his thoughts are taking.

We talk of other people who died suddenly, quickly. It can happen to anyone, the young bride of last year, why, even Agnelli's grandson, who was only thirty-eight.

"Thirty-three," Costanzo corrects, speaking up for the first time. "He was thirty-three. He went to America to be cured, but—*niente*. You know Agnelli? The head of Ferrari, the car that Schumacher drives."

19

When I told Richard and Libby about my grass-cutting, Libby said, "Be careful, be very careful, there are snakes!" Then she said: "Are you letting Renato have your hay? He could jolly well cut the grass around the house for you." I told them this had always been our arrangement with Costanzo, and that the hay had passed from Costanzo to Renato without our having been consulted.

"We'll sort him out. I'll go with you and talk to him. I've already had words with Renato recently, I'll tell you about it some day..."

But I rather think I should talk to Renato myself. I've been pacing around, trying to figure out what I will say. My little speech goes something like this: "My parents had an agreement with Costanzo that he could take our hay, and in return he did certain jobs at Querceto, for example cutting the grass around the house. Since you take our hay now, let's make a new agreement..."

But all of this seems too long and complicated. I'm afraid I'll lose my nerve... I call Libby and ask her advice. She says she might approach it more casually: "Would it be too much to ask that from now on, when you take the hay you cut the grass around the house as well?"

Oh, Libby is good! I will say it just like that.

I'm scared of Renato, that's what it is. I'm afraid of being turned down with my proposal, that it will not have the desired outcome. He is a formidable character. And I'm not used to asserting myself or standing up to people. My instinct is to assume a humble pose.

I think about how it is that Renato is so powerful. He is not a bad person. All the foreigners like him; they compete over who can be his closest friend. Look at Wenzel, so proud to be serving Renato's wine, despite the cows and the flies, or Ziegmann, quarreling with Wenzel on his behalf. Or Libby, so quick to forgive him. Even I can't help liking Renato. I don't want to be at odds with him.

And it's done. I made my little proposal, blushing and stumbling over my words. Lorenzo was there, looking on from a distance. Renato turned to Lorenzo, as if to say he was the one I should be addressing.

Lorenzo said a single word: "When?"

"Whenever you have time." Then I started

retreating, saying I hoped it wouldn't be too much work, thanking them profusely...

Early the next morning, at seven on the dot, I am awakened by the din of a motor just under my window. I throw open the shutters. This is a machine twice as big as Costanzo's. The noise is deafening. Wielding it is a man I don't know, with a face mask, goggles, and big noise-mufflers over his ears, his bare legs white with dust. I should have known Renato and Lorenzo wouldn't do this menial labor. They've delegated it to someone else. I throw on clothes (my hair is sticking out in the worst way) and go down to face the situation. I can't even open the door because he's mowing right in front of it, so I open the window instead.

The motor stops. The goggles are lifted.

His name is Marino. He has blue eyes and a kind, wrinkled face. He says Lorenzo gave him this job to do. Perhaps Lorenzo also told him to start at seven, under the bedroom window?

It turns out he is the one who is using our little field below the bake house to plant vegetables. Presumably it was Lorenzo who gave him permission.

He tells me that he is retired from road construction; the field is his weekend pastime. Beans and potatoes. "I'll do a good cleanup here," he says, smiling. He gestures a wide arc all the way to the oak tree. We agree that he'll take out the brambles but leave the broom standing.

He works without stopping for two, three hours. I go out at intervals to offer him coffee, juice, water; to this last offer he says, "No, not now," which at least is a concession that "maybe later."

"I'm doing my work," he says.

He wasn't joking. By the end of the morning, the whole area around the house is shorn, nothing left but stubble.

In the afternoon, Lorenzo comes to survey the job. He walks around, sternly looking everything over. "Where did he dump the grass?" he wants to know.

It's all perfectly amicable. We are both acting very adult. And of course we are adults—the next generation. But I still feel as though we were children, awkward and trying to look tall, stretching our necks like a couple of giraffes.

We shyly exchange a few words of conversation.

As we're standing there, Renato comes driving up the hill in his old Fiat Panda with Marino. They are going to mend the fence above the hay field. Lorenzo takes off on his moped. I tell Renato and Marino how pleased I am, how Marino did much more than was necessary, I'll feel so much safer from vipers.

Then I wave goodbye. I'm going over to La Croce to see Silvana.

"Tell her to come over here," Renato says. "Tell her Renato is here, too."

I phone her and she says she'll be right over. When she still hasn't come after ten minutes, I decide to go meet her halfway. But she hasn't even left the house. She seems to be hesitating fearfully on the threshold, her cardigan over her arm. She worries that her face is dirty from working in the garden. We walk back together.

"Oh, Renato!"

"Silvana!"

There is a palpable constraint in their meeting. I don't understand it. Maybe there has been a falling-out between the two families? Does that explain Silvana's hesitation to come? I have the impression they haven't talked to each other in a long time.

"Eh, Renato, one job more, one job less..." Silvana looks around. I suddenly feel bad because it is so much more extensive a mowing than Costanzo ever did.

I urge them to come inside. Marino doesn't want to because—looking at his watch—he's promised to be home at 4:30. "Only five minutes," I say. He gives in. We sit around the table in the kitchen. Everyone has a little orange juice mixed with water, and I pass around a plate of cookies.

And then it's a bit like an explosion. Without any preliminary, Silvana and Renato fall into an intense discussion, which moves so quickly that I only understand a fraction. Marino tries to put in a word here and there, but they pay no attention to him. It's all about springs and land boundaries up in the woods, some piece of land has been sold and it's not certain whether a spring is on this side or that—do you know that row of trees, and that little ditch, those trees are mine, but the cabin belongs to Squilloni...

The similarity between aunt and nephew at this moment is striking. They both have the same fierce energy in speaking. Silvana is transformed. She has laid down her gentle wifely guise and become a tycoon, a general, a leader of men. There is a sense of urgency, as if they were taking advantage of a rare opportunity. Then, just as suddenly, the conversation comes to an end, and Silvana gets up to go. She says goodbye to Renato in an affectionate, lingering tone, as if to a relative living in another part of the country.

Within this universe only a few kilometers squared, there are perhaps greater distances than I had imagined.

Poor Marino: it's 4:30 by the time they go outside again, and the fence still has to be mended.

20

"How is your work coming along?" Libby prods me.

"OK so far," I tell her. In reality, it is not progressing well at all.

"The thing about you people who write," she says, "is that you don't really have anything to show for your time. For what it's worth, when a painter goes into the studio, after three hours you can go in and see what he's done. You—how do I know if you're actually doing something or not?"

I laugh uneasily.

"I had a friend who wanted to write a book," she goes on. "She went to great trouble to have one evening each week free from her family. She found herself sitting behind the closed door at her computer, not knowing what to write. She admitted to me that whenever she heard her husband's footsteps approaching, she'd clatter her fingers on the keyboard so that it would sound as if she were working."

Richard smiles. "I can just see it. Every time you hear Ziegmann out there talking to the tree, you start hitting the keyboard."

We are once again sitting on their terrace. Richard points out the geranium pots on the ledge, where, he says, the lizards make their homes.

"When I come out first thing in the morning, I can see them all inside their pots."

There is a freedom about the Parkers' existence that I envy. Fundamentally apart from society, it seems to me like a large and very cozy tent pitched in the wilderness. Unlike the Germans, who idealize the peasant culture and imagine that they are assimilating themselves by putting oil on their bread instead of butter, Libby and Richard, who live here year-round, have no such illusions. They know the local people well but don't imitate them; they speak Italian fluently but without much effort at pronunciation. They keep teatime and are forever nostalgic for foods like hot dogs and peanut butter.

"We don't really live in Italy," Libby said to me once. "Let's face it, we're fish out of water here."

I know that the Parkers are a puzzle to Silvana and Costanzo, who wonder what they could possibly be doing from morning to night, particularly Richard, who after all is a man and does not have to do housework. Silvana asked me, in careful phrasing, "Does he suffer from a malady of the nerves?" They had obviously discussed it and come up with this idea. Costanzo watched my face and then, anticipating my reaction, sternly corrected her: "No, no, it's just his *character.*"

"He is a painter," I told them.

They both nodded knowingly. Amedeo was a painter, until he died from drink.

But even as I said it, I thought to myself, does Richard actually paint anymore? Will his studio ever be finished?

There is a mystery about Richard. I don't understand him either. If he wants to eat peanut butter, why doesn't he go back to America for a visit? He says he has never once been back since he left thirty years ago. What about his family? Doesn't he want to see them again? Whenever I ask him these questions, he gives me the same response: "Not in this lifetime."

Maybe he has committed some crime? Is he a wanted man?

I decide to take a different approach. I ask him how it was that he came to Italy. To my surprise, he is quite forthcoming.

He joined the military after graduating from high school because he wanted to see something of the world. After being stationed in Kentucky for three months he was sent to Germany. Once there, he saved up all his money and vacation time, because he'd heard that as a soldier you could fly anywhere for free if you went to the airport and put your name on a list. As

177

soon as his first leave came up, he went and put his name on a list for Paris. But there were no seats, and he returned to the base, disappointed, twenty-four hours of his vacation wasted. The next day he put his name on a list for the first available flight, and ended up bound for Libya. "When we landed in Tripoli, I looked out the window and saw nothing but sand and date palms. I knew immediately that this wasn't the place for me. I just wanted to fly back on the same plane. But they told me it wasn't possible; I'd have to get off and put my name on a waiting list for another flight. They left me there."

He had sat on the plane next to a British officer. This man now offered to show him the nightlife in Tripoli. They went to a bar run by a very fat old Italian woman.

"There were no other women at all besides her. There was nothing going on. The English guy saw that I wasn't impressed, and he told me that when he wanted to have a really good time, he'd go out with the Canadians. The English were forbidden to fight with the Arabs, but the Canadians would go into town wearing what they called bib-and-tuckers, and when the Arabs made fun of them, then they would get into fights."

As Richard and his friend walked back from the

bar to the hotel, every time they passed an Arab the Englishman would call out, "Mohammed!" "They always respond," he explained to Richard, "because they're all named Mohammed."

Libby is appalled. She is obviously hearing this story for the first time. "But what kind of an Englishman was this? I mean, what drawer was he out of?"

After that, Richard left the army and traveled all over Europe, working odd jobs. He began to study classical painting, first in Seville and then in Florence, where he met Libby.

"I remember the first time he invited me to his tiny apartment for dinner," Libby says. "There was something that looked like a sofa, covered with a blanket. I sat down on it and it was very hard, so I said, 'This feels like it's made out of bricks.' And Richard said, 'That's because it is.' I lifted a corner of the blanket, and that was really all it was. A pile of bricks."

She looks very happy at this memory.

"As for me, well, you see, after college I was working for a London publishing house. All the nice men there were gay, but I didn't know that initially. In fact, I was rather sweet on one of them, and he really led me down the garden path. We did romantic things together! Then one day I invited him to a party at my mother's house. I was proudly introducing my handsome suitor, and he chose that of all occasions to tell me he was gay. So there I was, twenty-four and with no prospects. Of course, the hunting types I met at my mother's house in the country didn't appeal to me at all. And then my grandmother took me on a holiday to Florence—"

"Where you were picked up by an Italian," Richard interjects.

Libby laughs, blushing. "After that, it was goodbye, England."

But all this still doesn't solve the mystery of why Richard won't return to the United States.

"Speaking of Ziegmann," Libby says.

The Parkers have invited me for dinner, to meet some of the people they have been telling me about.

"We wanted to invite Sabina, but she's taken off suddenly for Hamburg, poor thing, and of course it's one or the other, so we're having Claudio instead."

The guest list also includes a Norwegian named Dag Jensen, his American wife Rachel, and Bonnie, an Englishwoman whom I've met before.

"We are pretty sure that Jensen smuggles

weapons and stolen art. Although of course that is not what he says. But Brigitte Mandelbaum worked for him briefly as a secretary, and she says it was obvious from the letters she typed."

Bonnie lives in a house on the other side of the hill, beyond Spazzavento. Libby tells me her story again. She used to be married to a man named George, a veterinarian who worked at a pig farm near Vigliano. "He always smelled terribly of pigs." Contrary to their usual habit, Libby and Richard bought a local paper one day to find out about an announced strike. That paper carried a tiny notice that the British consulate was looking for an agricultural attaché. They gave the snippet to George, and he got the job.

"So you see, what happened was our fault in a way. If he'd stayed with the pigs, no woman would have gone after him, smelling like that. But instead, he took this job and shaped up. He met his first floozy at the agricultural fair in Verona, and then later he went off with another one from the consulate. She was *older* than Bonnie. But you know, Bonnie never cooked, she never made him comfortable and was always nagging at him; and then he went off with this marvelous cook."

The evening comes. The guests arrive. Ziegmann shakes my hand with cold formality, as if he

181

didn't remember having met me before. We sit on the terrace under the fluttering awning, sipping gin-and-tonics and nibbling appetizers.

I look surreptitiously at Dag Jensen. His appearance is very disappointing, not how I would have imagined a smuggler. He is a small man with blond hair curving upward from his forehead in a stiff tuft, like the comic figure Tintin. The shape of the tuft is repeated in his upturned nose. Thrusting his chest forward, he speaks loudly in sudden rapid volleys, like someone who has learned to overcome a stutter.

His wife Rachel, a petite woman with dyed black hair wound into a chignon, is talking about their property just outside a place called Sagginale. Hannibal is supposed to have come through there, hence the village emblem is an elephant. "It's thrilling to think that Hannibal might have camped right where our house stands now!" When they dug up their field several years ago to build the swimming pool, they found what seemed to be pre-Roman artifacts.

I can't help exclaiming: "A swimming pool!" Nobody hears me but Richard, who, because he says so little, hears everything.

"The place is just so rich with history. We are becoming amateur archaeologists. I'm even convinced there was a medieval tower or castle on our property that Barbarossa pulled down. I've been going to the archives in Florence to find evidence, but I haven't found it yet."

Dag says, "We dug up a stone that we've been told was probably a tool for cutting meat off the bone." He laughs a manly laugh which suggests that he likes to imagine the meat raw, dripping with blood.

I give myself a push. "You must have plenty of water then, if you have a swimming pool."

"Oh, we're attached to the municipal water line. We're part of civilization down there."

Ziegmann bursts out: "A swimming pool is an abomination!" His face is red. "How can you build a swimming pool! Amidst the olive groves! Amidst the corn fields!"

Secretly, I can't help agreeing with him.

"You don't *own* the history," he sputters. "We don't *own* anything here. We are merely *custodians*. Our role is to *preserve*, not to *ruin*."

This is not a good beginning. Libby turns to Bonnie, who until now has been silent, sitting back in her chair with a little smile that seems to say she doesn't mind being left out. She is a tall, attractive, fair-haired woman with a pageboy haircut and eyebrows arched almost to points from tension pulling them upwards.

"Bonnie, how have you been doing?"

"Oh, I'm just listening, lapping it up. I like hearing other people talk. It seems all I do is work these days, so I have nothing much to say."

I ask about her work, remembering vaguely that she is a nurse. From being completely silent, she launches without apparent effort into a monologue, talking about the two boys she takes care of in a private home.

"Young men, really, one has to be realistic about this. They're seventeen now, Aldo and Pietro. Their father is a doctor, very nice man although unfortunately it's his wife I deal with mostly. They're completely crippled. Brain damage, too, poor things. They can't read, and they're not much good at arithmetic. But they can do everything on the computer."

She has an oddly flat manner of speaking, which seems to express only fatigued indifference. It contrasts so strongly with what she is saying that I have to fight a mounting impulse to laugh.

She drones on bleakly. "Although they're twins, they're complete opposites. Aldo is wise beyond his years, while Pietro has remained a little child. They're both terrifically attached to me, as I am to them. The horrible thing is that it's only going to get worse. It could go on like this for years, or then again they could die young."

Everyone else has fallen silent. I happen to glance at Richard, who rolls his eyes. I hold my breath and avoid looking at him after this.

"I've never seen such a tragic family. In the past fifteen months they've had four deaths: the grandmother, the mother's father, the brother-in-law's sister, and an aunt."

"Were they all in the same car when it crashed?" Richard asks.

"No," Bonnie replies wearily. "At least then it would have been *one* tragedy, and it would have been over with. But they died in dribs and drabs."

A small noise escapes me. Libby looks at me sternly. Rachel asks what the boys' disease is. Bonnie says that she can never remember its name, but that it begins with a "D." Everyone begins searching for words starting with "D," until Bonnie, with a worried look, says that perhaps, after all, it begins with "P," upon which they go back to talking about other things, leaving her once again alone.

To make amends, I say: "Libby tells me you have all kinds of animals at your house." This change of topic cheers Bonnie up, and she lists the animals she has, two of each, like on Noah's Ark.

185

I am vaguely aware that Dag has begun to stare at the two of us.

"I feel certain I've seen you before," he remarks to Bonnie, interrupting her. "At the British consulate."

"My ex-husband works there," Bonnie replies, blushing.

Libby stands up briskly. "Shall we go inside for dinner now? Richard, please make sure no one trips over that step."

We are seated around the long, festively laid table. The wine is poured into goblets that look as if they had been taken from an eighteenth-century still-life. At one end of the table the former conversation is resumed, with Ziegmann fulminating against foreigners while Libby and Rachel maintain that but for the foreigners, most of the houses in Tuscany, not to mention the entire economy, would be in ruins.

Dag looks at Bonnie and is reminded of the British consulate.

"Richard, have I ever told you why Rachel and I are no longer invited to the Queen's birthday parties at Villa Spellman?"

"No, you haven't."

"Well, it happened like this. A few years ago, the last time we were invited, I was talking to the wife of the French consul. I said to her, 'I find you very attractive.' And she said to me, 'But *you* are very attractive.' And her husband was fucking listening to the whole thing. So we were never invited again. Not, you understand, because *I* said *she* was attractive, but because *she* said *I* was attractive."

Again the manly laugh. I glance over at his wife and am startled to find Rachel staring at me fixedly. I try in vain to recall my facial expressions in the moments immediately preceding.

I ask Dag: "What is it that you do?"

"Oh, this and that. I'm an entrepreneur. Import-export, mostly."

The evening goes on—the relationship between the church and the Mafia. Ziegmann makes pounding motions with his fist to drive a point home. Libby looks embarrassed. At one point, Richard reaches over and gently removes a bit of mashed potato that has somehow found its way into my hair. "Were you planning to take this home with you?"

"Spastics!"

This word, uttered in a loud voice by Bonnie, brings all conversation to a halt.

"I've finally remembered what they're called. Spastics."

Silence.

"Perhaps we should have our dessert."

21

A strong wind has come up. It makes the shutters slam violently, rustles in the giant lilac bush and the small trees below the house, pushes a constantly changing arrangement of white clouds across the deep blue sky. I see a lumber truck going up the road toward Castellina, but the roar of the wind drowns out the sound of its motor.

In the afternoon the wind subsides and it starts to rain. The first drops are huge, falling singly with a big splat on the stones of the terrace, each making a spot four centimeters in diameter. The earth starts to give off a deep odor. By late afternoon it is raining in earnest. The house is enveloped in mist, nothing but whiteness visible outside the windows, as if I were in the center of a cloud. Which in fact I probably am.

It continues to rain into the night, and the next morning it is still raining. I think that now, at least, Silvana and Costanzo, who have done nothing but complain about the drought since the day I arrived, should be happy. But when I go to see them they make worried, dissatisfied faces.

"It's not enough," Silvana says. "It's too late. This year is a disaster."

That seems ungrateful, considering the way the water is coming down. It's strange that they should care so much since they no longer cultivate any land except for the vegetable garden, which can be watered by hand. Probably their concern is simply an old habit. And Silvana's grumbling, I suspect, is really a superstitious ploy to prevent the rain from being stopped again prematurely. If so, it's successful. The rain continues. It makes the house gloomy and damp. I find myself staring out the windows, mesmerized by the steady downward motion. I eat my meals indoors; for the first time, I feel lonely. I feel trapped by that relentless downpouring.

By the third day, I'm almost out of milk and bread; I have no yogurt left. But I'm afraid to venture out with the car. I envision myself stuck with churning tires in some patch of road that has turned to mud.

I finally give myself a push and go. The Uno slithers on the path but goes forward. The gray sky hangs low over the landscape, which seems to duck down into itself. There is something forlorn and depressing about the isolated farmhouses. I picture the inhabitants huddled inside, trying to keep dry.

In Vigliano at least there are people walking about, carrying umbrellas; in town it's as easy as that. The square is almost as busy as ever. My spirits are lifted. I throw my trash into the big dumpster, get money at the bank, and buy an extra gas cylinder for the stove. I have an ice cream and stock up on groceries at the Co-op, tomatoes and cheese and fat fennel bulbs. I decide that I will try to make a fire in the wood stove in the kitchen to cheer me as I cook.

As I drive back up the hill, there are no dogs to chase me at Riaccio, and I almost miss them. I see two horses on a field, one brown, one black, standing in rigid, unnatural poses on either side of a small tree. They are near the tree but not quite underneath it, as if caught midway between their instinct to seek shelter and their experience showing it to be useless.

On the morning of the fifth day, a blond-gray mouse runs out into the middle of the kitchen and just looks at me, with round, shining eyes.

I am filling water into a cooking pot when the stream from the faucet suddenly stops. Without fanfare it diminishes to a trickle and then nothing.

In a sickening flash I realize I've allowed myself to grow careless. When was the last time I checked the cisterns? Until now, whenever I thought about it, all I needed to do was listen carefully to hear the water dripping in. Ironically, the rain would have made it impossible to hear that small sound.

There is an old cob-webby pair of rubber boots in the *stalla*. Before putting them on I shake them out vigorously, banging them against the wall in case a scorpion is hiding inside. As I unlock the door to the *stallina* I hear the little pump laboring because I haven't turned off the kitchen faucet. That can mean only one thing. The cisterns are empty.

I go back inside and close the faucet and pull the electrical plug on the pump.

I am hungry, so I continue making my supper using bottled water. My mind is racing. What can be the problem now? Surely the spring can't be dry, with all this rain. I am angry at myself because I allowed myself to be lulled into a false sense of security. But underneath, I know I've been expecting this moment all along.

Three-quarters of an hour later, I am on the phone talking to Luca Fabbri.

It's been about twenty years since I last saw Fabbri. He was our builder. My parents found him after a series of other builders whose work was sloppy, though their smiles were winning. Fabbri was different, a serious, quiet man, a perfectionist. He had strong opinions about material and proportion and about not charging clients, even if they were foreigners, for more than the time spent actually working.

His number is in one of the phone books I picked up from Alessandra. And he seems happy to hear from me: yes, certainly he remembers, a beautiful house, Querceto. No, it's not crazy of me to have called him. In this type of situation you need an outsider, someone whose interests are not connected to any of the people involved. He will bring his own *idraulico*, a good man, completely trustworthy.

"We'll look into it," he says. "Don't worry. Do you have enough water for tonight?"

The next morning the rain has finally stopped. It's a beautiful clear day. The sun is shining and a thick mist is welling up out of the valley.

Punctually at nine o'clock, a car appears from the woods at the bottom of the hill. A shiny black car, utterly unfit for the road. They will have to walk up from Casabassa, I think. But instead, I watch as the car maneuvers, turns around, and proceeds up the hill backward. Front-wheel drive. By the time it reaches the top, its shiny finish—it is a BMW—is spattered from top to bottom with mud. Fabbri climbs out of the passenger seat.

"Buongiorno!"

I've never been happier to see a person again. He seems hardly changed to me after all this time, neat and brisk, with his round face and close-shaven hair: only perhaps a bit thinner. I can tell from his broad smile that I look quite a bit changed to him.

"This is my associate, Gianfranco Generini."

More handshaking. Generini looks the opposite of Fabbri, slightly overweight and all ramshackle, with an uneven haircut and ill-fitting clothes, though he seems to have put on his Sunday best. He hands me his business card. *Generini Gianfranco,* I read. *Thermo-sanitary Systems, Air Conditioning, Garden Irrigation, Water Games.* Water games? No, *Giochi d'Acqua* must be "play of water," as in ornamental fountains. Doubtfully, I look at Generini's shoes, which are black and shiny, as his car formerly was. Fabbri is clad in strong workman's boots, and I am wearing an old pair of sneakers.

"Please come in. Thank you so much for coming at short notice. As I explained…" I've set the table with coffee cups and a plate of packaged apricot tarts. The tarts look unappetizing: their edges are so clean that they seem fake, as if they won't crumble. And I'd forgotten about sugar; at the last minute I managed to scrape together some ancient lumps from the bottom of a container.

As I carry the coffee pot to the table, the lid, which belongs to some other pot and doesn't fit accurately, falls into the coffee with a resonant *plop*.

When we are finally seated — my two guests are taking tiny, polite sips of sugarless coffee and not touching the pastries — I explain everything as best I can from the beginning. How the spring belongs to three houses, four if Renato's cow shed is counted; how, when I first arrived and had no water, Renato said it was because a storm had dislodged the tube leading from a stream to the spring; and how we went up there with Landi and he moved the tube around a bit and afterward I had water again.

"Renato also said that the people at Castellina, the house above Pruneto, are tapping into our spring through their well."

Fabbri and Generini look at each other for a few moments.

"*C'è del buio*," Fabbri says finally. "There is darkness."

"It does happen sometimes," Generini says thoughtfully, "when a spring doesn't give very much water, that people will feed water from a stream into the collecting basin. But I want to have a look for myself."

"Why don't we go have a look right now," Fabbri suggests. He seems eager to get up from the table. I suddenly realize that I've forgotten to remove the chair with the broken seat. All this time, he must have been perching uncomfortably on its edge.

I offer the use of the Uno, but Generini insists on taking his BMW. "It doesn't mind the mud."

"*C'è del buio*," Fabbri repeats as we roll very slowly and carefully down the hill. "There's something strange going on. You can't trust people around here. I remember when I was working on your house, pieces of wood that I had taken out of the old roof would disappear and I'd see them a few days later as part of a fence."

"Well, I certainly think Costanzo is completely honest," I say.

Fabbri shakes his head. "They were in Costanzo's fence."

"Perhaps he thought you weren't using them anymore." I think of the discarded highway billboards that make up the Donatis' hut in the wood, and his crude fences, made from whatever materials he can scavenge. He probably thought one or two staves wouldn't be missed. "Costanzo is a good person."

"You can't trust any of them," Fabbri insists. I am surprised by his attitude toward the peasants, from whom he is probably separated by only one generation. "But you're absolutely right," he goes on, "if you're saying Renato's the one to watch out for. Just look at his farm. He must have a hundred cows, and yet his parents were sharecroppers like everyone else. You don't get that rich without being *furbo*. I wouldn't be surprised if he were tapping into the line somewhere, taking all the water for his cattle."

Generini is silent during this exchange, looking attentively about him.

"The house where the spring is located is up this way?" he asks.

"Yes, just a little further. I'm not exactly sure where the spring is…" I am suddenly worried about trespassing onto the Cavinis' property.

Generini stops the car. "What's this?"

We are less than a hundred meters from the gate of Pruneto. The road loops around after that to Castellina, which is directly above us on the hill. Generini is pointing at a cement container with a circular lid in the center, surrounded by brambles, a few meters away from the road.

"I don't know."

Generini turns off the motor and goes to look,

without waiting to see if we are following. He plunges recklessly through the mud in his new shoes and within seconds they are unrecognizable, completely coated in brown.

He lifts the lid.

"It's a well."

"Christine! Christine!" Libby's voice wails down from above like a siren. She is leaning over the parapet. "What on earth are you doing?"

"Looking for our spring," I shout back. "I have no water!"

I feel at a disadvantage because I have to cast my voice upwards while Libby can simply drop hers down.

"Who are these people?"

"I'll explain later!" I shout.

Fabbri and Generini follow this exchange with incredulous expressions, as if amazed that we can understand each other.

"That one's ours," Libby's voice sings out. "That's nothing to do with you!"

Even over this distance, I can tell she sounds annoyed.

"OK, sorry!"

I turn to Generini. "She says that's their well and has nothing to do with our spring." Generini looks up toward Castellina, where the parapet is now empty, and then over at Pruneto. He seems to be calculating something in his mind.

I add: "She's my friend."

"Well, let's go see the spring then."

Fabbri and I walk the short piece and wait by the gate for Generini to pull up his mud-spattered car.

"It doesn't look like anybody's home," Fabbri remarks, doubtfully eyeing the warning plaque illustrated with a German shepherd's head.

Generini scarcely dignifies the plaque with a glance. Splashing through a deep puddle at the side of the gate, he finds a place where the barbed wire sags a little and holds it down with his foot for us to climb over. He is clearly the leader of our little group now. Despite his citified clothes, he seems in his true element here. It's remarkable to see the change in Fabbri, who is deferring to him completely.

As we enter the forbidden garden I glance around, hoping to see something of interest. I imagine the Cavinis returning on the weekend, walking down their path unaware that it has been trodden by strangers. Generini has already found a little fountain set into the low garden wall. He turns the faucet, which emits a rustle trickle into the tiny basin. We all watch the trickle for a few moments, then Generini, without a word, closes the faucet again. Climbing up on the wall, which separates the garden from the wooded area rising behind it, he walks about ten paces into the trees.

"Here it is."

Fabbri and I scramble to follow him. There, in the ground, are two cement containers less than a meter apart, one larger, one smaller.

"This is the collecting basin," he says, pointing to the larger one, "and this is where it comes out of the ground."

He lifts the cover to the receptacle that protects the spring. I feel a surge of excitement. Our spring! This is it! I can actually see water coming out of the rock.

"And this here is the tube coming in from the stream."

"So?" Fabbri shifts impatiently from one foot to the other. "Is there any water?"

"There's plenty."

In fact, there is a big puddle around the first basin, while the second one is empty. Generini has his hand on a lever on the outside of the collecting basin and is moving it from one position to the other.

He turns to me: "This is where they could turn the water off on the rest of you, if they wanted to. But it was open."

Then, to my dismay, he lies down full-length on the sodden ground and sticks his head into the first basin. He reaches in with his right arm, then pulls it out again.

"Give me a stick."

Fabbri and I watch in silence as he maneuvers the branch inside the hole, then throws it aside and uses his arm again.

We all hear the sound of water splashing into the collecting basin.

"The tube was stopped up," he says when he finally stands up. I can hardly bear to look at him: covered in mud from head to toe. "The tube leading from one to the other. It happens."

"That was all? A stopped-up tube?"

"Now we'll go back to the house and see if the water is coming."

On the way down Generini drives even more slowly than he did on the way up. He keeps peering to the left and right of the road as if searching for something. At one point, he stops the car and gets out, takes a few steps in one direction and in another, then gets back in and drives on.

Fifty meters, and he stops again. Querceto is just up the hill on our left. We're not far from Casabassa. Generini turns the engine off. "What is it?" Fabbri asks.

Generini gets out and walks over to the side of the road.

"It looks like someone's been digging here recently." He indicates a spot in the embankment with his toe. "This must be about where your tube goes up to your house. It runs right by the side of the road the whole way."

Fabbri and I look at the spot at which he is pointing. Perhaps the grass is a little sparser? It takes either imagination or knowledge to infer recent digging.

But Fabbri catches on. "Whose shed is that?" On the right side of the road there is an aluminum shed that I've never particularly noticed. It's a shed like so many others, a bit ugly so that one blocks it out of one's mind.

"I have no idea."

Once again we have to climb over a barbed-wire fence. This time the warning sign reads: "Private Property. Trespassing Forbidden. Violators Will Be Prosecuted." As if to make up for this unfriendliness, the cow that pokes its head out from the shed gives us a welcoming moo.

I find the cement box, well hidden behind a clump of bushes. The round lid lifts off easily. Inside is a shiny red spigot.

"Turn it," Generini says.

I turn it. Immediately there is a gurgling of water in the black rubber tube, and seconds later there comes from inside the shed the muted thunder of water splashing into an aluminum trough. The cow, which has been curiously watching our activity, is startled into stepping all the way out of the shed. A second cow sticks its head out in consternation. Following an unconscious suggestion, the first cow lets out a long stream of urine, and a moment later, the same sound can be heard echoing from just inside the shed.

I turn the spigot back to the "off" position.

22

Our discovery has confirmed Fabbri's worst suspicions about the peasants.

"I told you so," he says. "It's an *attacco abusivo* — an illegal attachment. I'm sure Renato is behind this. Are you sure that isn't his shed?"

"I'm not sure of anything."

We are sitting on the terrace at Querceto, waiting to see if the water will come back. Generini has said it might take a few minutes, given the altitude of the house. In checking the cistern, he noticed that the rubber floater which closes the valve when the cistern is full is cracked, and water has seeped inside. He is repairing it as we wait. By means of a tubular plant stem inserted into the tiny crack, he is patiently emptying out the water.

"That tap wasn't turned on," he remarks.

"Still," Fabbri insists. "It's a big problem. It's illegal. Did you see how carefully it was hidden? Those sneaky bastards! What if we hadn't found it? You know, don't you," turning to me, "that if they keep on taking the water unchallenged for twelve years, they acquire the right to it. There wouldn't be a thing you could do about it. It's called usucaption."

"But what can I do about it now?"

"I'm not sure that we've gotten to the bottom of the problem," Generini says. "We should retrace the entire length of the tube on foot."

Fabbri is silent. He doesn't seem happy at this suggestion. His wife will have lunch waiting.

"Perhaps we should do that another time," I suggest. I contemplate Generini, who looks as if he'd been rolling around full-length in a mud puddle. Underneath this unassuming exterior is a passion for getting to the bottom of things. He is now spreading glue on the crack in the floater to seal it up. Any other plumber would simply have sold me a new floater.

"I think I hear something," Fabbri says.

The first drops, pushed along by the weight of the water behind them, have finally climbed the steep hill to the house and are falling into the cistern.

"*Niente*," says Fabbri when I thank them. "We'll send the bill later on."

Left to myself, I feel a kind of heady excitement, which builds up pressure because I have no one to talk to. I move about the house without much purpose, running up and down the stairs to expend energy, repeating

Fabbri's words, *C'è del buio*, out loud with a dramatic intonation. There is darkness, mystery. An *attacco abusivo*!

Gradually the excitement drains out of me, and I feel disheartened.

Libby answers the phone on the first ring. She must have been waiting for my call.

"The shed belongs to a man named Adriani," she says after listening to my account. "Cesare Adriani. He's a mechanic. He owns a big garage down in Borgo. He must have bought the land from Renato. He keeps a few cows up here just for the fun of it, I think."

I don't ask how she knows this; Libby knows everything. What's more, I recognize the name. When I was young and we were stuck on the road once, it was Cesare Adriani who fixed the problem. It was something small, and he didn't charge us for the repair.

"It's something to be taken seriously at any rate," Libby says. "I'm sure Renato put Adriani up to it. He's probably getting something in return, that's the way it works around here. The thing to do is to see a *geometra*. Geometers in Italy don't just measure the land, you know. They're legal experts. We can give you the name of a good man in Borgo."

I keep checking the water at fifteen-minute

intervals all afternoon. Before I go to bed it's still coming in, a steady succession of drops that stop just short of being a trickle. The cistern is almost half full.

In the night I dream that I am following Generini, who is following the course of the tube. We are walking along slowly, our eyes fixed to the ground, peering intently into the grass. We want to get to the bottom of the matter, but our detective work is difficult because there are many tubes branching off below ground, a never-ending web. We are trying to find the secret undercurrents and the distant, hidden sources of everything that happens on the surface. It's one of those interminable dreams: we go on and on.

The next day I go to see Stefano Pieri, the *geometra* in Borgo to whom Libby has referred me. His office is in a nice square office building. The sign by his door reads, "Agrarian Expert and Geometer." I have to wait for some time in a waiting room that smells of doctors' and dentists' practices.

At last Pieri ushers me in, giving me a piercing look just like a stern but kindly doctor. Gray hair, beard, horn-rimmed glasses. His desk is piled high with stacks of paper; on a separate table there is a state-of-the-art computer assembly. Mountains of file boxes occupy all the remaining space in the room.

Frowning and folding his hands in a thoughtful way, Pieri initiates the discussion by recapitulating what I've told him on the phone.

"It's a serious matter," he agrees. "Say you're taking a bath, you're covered with soap, and all of a sudden you have no water. What are you going to do? Run down the hill and ask this Adriani to close his faucet? That thing has actually happened to me."

He explains that he has a vacation house where he has a similar problem, with several people attaching themselves to his aqueduct at lower points, drawing off the water that is rightfully his.

"You basically have three choices. One, you simply cut the man off." He makes a chopping motion with his hand. "Let him see where he finds his water. If you want to be nice about it, you could offer him some alternatives—allow him, for instance, to take water from an overflow tube installed at the spring itself, or allow him to attach his tube near your house, with a valve that *you* control, but at a higher point so that he will get the water last.

"The second choice is to allow him to continue to use the attachment he has made, but to draw up an agreement for usufruct, properly notarized, whereby he pays each of the rightful proprietors of the spring, of which you have told me there are four, a yearly nominal sum for its use. Even as little as a thousand lire. This would prevent his acquiring the right to the water by usucaption. You say that there are at present only two cows, and that you are concerned about maintaining friendly relations with the local farmer, who probably had a hand in making the attachment or at least permitted it. In that case, this might be an acceptable solution, causing the least amount of disruption and bad feelings to all parties.

"Your third choice, finally, is to do nothing. This I would not advise."

Back at Querceto, I try to go over it all in my mind rationally, logically. But I find I can think only in images. I see Renato's closed, hostile face the day I went to visit them, and Costanzo's uncomfortable expression when I first brought up the subject of water. I hear Libby's high, annoyed voice telling me to keep away from their well. I hear Fabbri saying, *attacco abusivo*, in his precise way. And then I picture Pieri sitting in a small bathtub covered with soap.

A nice man, Pieri. It's good to have someone like

him on one's side. He agreed with Fabbri that Adriani's attachment must be taken seriously. Without water, there is no house.

Presumably, Adriani is also a nice man, who fixes cars and only wants to keep two cows in the country. But what if one day he decides to retire from fixing cars and acquire more cows? Then there will be nothing left for Querceto or Casabassa. I'm sure Wenzel would agree that this is a problem. And even Renato should agree, since he still has his cow shed at Casabassa. The thing that seems to make the most sense is for everyone involved to sign a contract, as Pieri suggested, allowing Adriani to keep his faucet for a nominal payment. It's something I could try, at any rate, to bring about.

But to do this, I would first have to confront Renato.

I'm crazy to think that it can be done amicably. How am I even going to bring it up? No one who has done something wrong reacts well to having it brought out in the open. The very fact of my having called an *idraulico* from the outside, instead of trusting Landi, might be taken as an act of war. I see Renato's face again, this time dressed in his best smile-for-the-foreigners. Fabbri had the same word for him as Libby: *furbo*. Shrewd and cunning.

Doubts assail me. Isn't it a bit late in the day? And after all, I'm alone here, a woman. What can I hope to achieve?

I hear voices over at La Croce and I feel differently toward them than in the past. Costanzo and Silvana must have known about the attachment all along.

I walk over one day in the late afternoon; I haven't seen them in more than a week. Costanzo is standing by Domenico's house talking to a young man I've never seen before. They seem to be engaged in some sort of business transaction, and Costanzo greets me with only a brief nod, as if he scarcely knew me. I am stung to the quick. Perhaps he doesn't want to be seen to be on friendly terms with me? The young man assumes a genial expression and raises his voice unnaturally to say, "Are you on vacation?"

Seeing me hesitate as if to turn back, Costanzo perhaps feels some compunction. "Silvana is in the house," he says. So I go on. Silvana is in the midst of mopping the floor furiously. "Come in, stay," she says. "I'm almost finished." It looks as if the mop itself were having a convulsive fit and she were being dragged along helplessly behind it as it races around the corners.

We sit chatting for about ten minutes. Costanzo comes in and is quite friendly again. It turns out the man he was talking to was merely checking the electricity counters.

While we are talking about something else, Costanzo suddenly remembers he has to take his pill.

"Silvana, bring me my pill." He says it in an undertone, very quickly, a secret sub-text to our formal, official conversation.

She doesn't respond; she is talking to me.

After a minute: "Is the pill coming?"

... "Silvana!"

Silvana puts water to boil on the stove for their supper, and I leave shortly thereafter.

23

The weather stays fine. The water keeps coming in. For all intents and purposes, the problem has been fixed, a matter of a clogged tube at the spring. I've become absorbed in working on my thesis, and have finally begun to make real progress. With all this, I've let the whole matter of Adriani's attachment fade gently out of my mind. Perhaps Pieri's words, "do nothing," were magic and have put a spell on me.

One morning, I am working with the window open when I hear Renato's sharp, gingery voice down at Casabassa. I hadn't planned to confront him, but suddenly the moment seems right. Maybe I just want an excuse to get away from my desk.

I walk down the hill. Lorenzo is there too.

"I wanted to talk to you," I say to Renato. "I didn't have water a few weeks ago. I called another *idraulico*, and we found a hidden attachment leading to that shed over there. Do you know about it?"

"What attachment?" he challenges defiantly.

Lorenzo disappears into the shed.

"I'll show you."

Together we walk over to the place that Generini discovered. Renato keeps up his act of not

212

knowing what I'm talking about, as if hoping for a miracle. Until the moment when I lift the lid and point to the shiny new tap. There is a shift as palpable as if the ground had suddenly tilted the other way.

Seeing Renato's face at that moment, I feel a flash of regret. I realize I'm not cut out to have the advantage of another person. It's a situation I've instinctively avoided all my life.

"I don't know anything about it."

If I had any doubt before, it's clear as day now that he had an active part in making or allowing the attachment.

I sense the need to stay firm.

"It's an *attacco abusivo*. I understand this shed and the cows in it belong to a man named Adriani. I've gone to see Pieri, the *geometra* in Borgo, about it."

"Yes, yes, I know Pieri." He looks crestfallen.

"I'm not saying that we should cut Adriani off. As long as he has only these two cows, I think there is enough for all of us. But we have to think of the future. What if one day he wants to buy ten more cows? There would be nothing left for us." I make a gesture suggesting our mutual interest. "Pieri says it can be done very simply, by means of a piece of paper that we all sign, preventing him from acquiring the right to the water by usucaption."

Relief dawns on Renato's face. But he is still wary. "What about the *tedesco* from Casabassa? And Cavini? They won't agree to this."

"I can ask Wenzel. He is a reasonable person. I think he will probably agree. And why don't you talk to Cavini?"

Renato's face clouds over again. "Cavini is not reasonable. We haven't talked in three years. Can't you talk to him? I have his phone number. We can call him together. I'll dial, you talk."

Renato wants to make the call as soon as possible. We agree that I will come to his house on Saturday afternoon, when the Cavinis are most likely to be at Pruneto.

On Saturday at five, I head down to Renato's farm. He has prepared things by placing the telephone on the kitchen table and beside it his impressive-looking ledger, which is larger in format than the phone book. The numbers in it are written almost an inch high, four or five to a page. Although the telephone lines were installed on the Fattoria ten years ago, making an official call is still something of a state occasion.

Alessandra stands in the background, having

greeted me with a little nod.

Renato picks up the receiver using only his thumb and first two fingers, and holds it at an odd angle away from his face. He looks at me as if for moral support as he dials the numbers. *"Pronto!* Montanari Renato here! I have *la tedesca* from Querceto here with me!" Renato is shouting, and I suppose the person on the other end is shouting too: that is why the receivers have to be held at a distance.

Renato listens, looking at Alessandra and me in turn, then cups his hand over the receiver. "That was his wife. She says she has to go get him. He's in the bathroom." A faint grin betrays his glee at having surprised Cavini in a humiliating position.

"Here, you talk to him."

What follows can barely be called a conversation. While I try to explain the situation, the voice at the other end interrupts me every other sentence with a gruff shout: *Who! What! What attachment! What Adriani! Cut him off! Nothing! I won't sign anything! I don't give a damn! Cut him off, I say!*

Dazed, I put the phone down.

"He refused. He said he doesn't even care about the spring because he's found another one all his own. But he still refused to sign anything."

"He's not a reasonable man."

"He thinks he's better than us," Alessandra says, "because he lives in Florence."

We leave it that I will write a letter to Wenzel. If he agrees to a contract, then maybe the next time he comes he can help us prevail upon Cavini. Perhaps his title, *dottore*, will carry some weight.

Renato offers me a *gocciolino*, and I accept. Lorenzo has gone to town with his *fidanzata*, but his huge baby picture stares down at us from its heavenly blue background as the three of us sip our wine.

I think to myself how strange it is: a little while ago, Renato was the enemy, and now we are standing together in his kitchen like conspirators. Doubtless it's true that he's *furbo*, and made or permitted Adriani's attachment in return for some favor or service. It's not by chance that he is the only successful farmer far and wide. But it seems to me that while it is possible, and justified, to be angry with him, it's also just as possible not to be.

II. *AUTUMN*

24

Autumn is coming. The weather is strange these days. One minute it's warm and mild, and the next there's a fierce cold wind, which makes the doors and shutters bang and the branches of the plum tree by the house scrape the gutter with a screeching sound. Silvana pulls her cardigan tightly about her as she stands in her doorway. "This wind, always this wind."

Approaching La Croce one evening, I come upon her at the gate to her animal pen, holding a huge dove-gray rabbit by the ears. It hangs heavily from her hand, eyes open, alert but not struggling. She smiles a little sheepishly when she sees me, perhaps thinking I'm squeamish at the thought of its slaughter. Or maybe she is embarrassed because I'm not invited to the feast.

I haven't seen the Donatis or the Parkers very much. I've been busy, writing and making trips into Florence to use the library. Once in a while it feels good to put on a dress and walk in the city. There will still be reference work to be done when I get home, quotations to be checked and footnotes added. But my argument is coming together; it's beginning to look solid. This should make me happy, but instead I feel wistful, as if I were reluctant to let it go.

The other day a group of people came walking up the hill, Florentines. I could tell at once they were city people. A woman and two men, the woman's excited voice audible from afar. "*Pietro, vieni!*" They wore hiking boots and carried backpacks; one of the men even had a walking stick. "Look, Pietro, this would be a house for you!" In the past, I would have withdrawn into the house to avoid being seen. Now, instead, I leaned out the window and waved: *Buonasera!* —to make them walk on.

But my presence didn't seem to bother them at all; they continued to stand and talk right in front of the house. They stopped just short of going onto the terrace in back. They took a few pictures of the view, then turned and walked back down the hill.

The woman's words made me indignant. I am surprised by the strength of my proprietary feeling. No, it's not a house for you, it's *mine!*

"But not for long..."

This is the same voice inside me that has begun saying every day, "This was the last summer. Soon I'll have to go home. The house will have to be sold."

Couldn't I just stay here, live here forever?

"How would you live?"

I could take jobs like Brigitte Mandelbaum. Pick zucchini, clean houses, whatever it takes.

"Would you want to do that?"

Why not?

For two days now I've been hearing the cries of the mule driver in the woods above the house— "Ah! Ah!" or "Ha! Ha!"—exhorting the animals along what must be only a narrow footpath. The Donatis have told me that they are mules, although when they appear now and then briefly between the branches, they look just like horses.

When I put the binoculars to my eyes, I can never find again that tiny incision in the green hillside where the logs are being piled up. I scan the woods until they become a blur, finally give up and locate the place again with my bare eyes. It's a narrow segment of white near the bottom of the dark-green hillside that rises to the northwest of Querceto, where the edge of the hill is met by the silhouette of the next hill behind it, a still darker shade of green.

That tiny scene fascinates me: the pile of logs, and the figure dressed in blue appearing and disappearing, working to pile them up from the place where, out of sight, the mules have dropped them down. Set upon a slim horizontal triangle, a sharp splinter of white in the vast blur of green, it's like a scene painted with a single brush-hair.

By contrast, the sound that the logs make as they fall into place is quite loud—a clear wooden ringing that seems close at hand, as if no distance at all separated them from me. It's louder than the cries of the mule driver, although the latter is passing at times much closer to the house. I catch glimpses of him between the branches, a man wearing what looks like a red skull cap. There seem to be six or seven mules.

I bring the binoculars up to my face again, this time taking care not to move my head or even my eyes at all. Again, I'm not quite there. But this time, by moving just a little bit, I find it. Now the scene fills out my whole view. The logs, though still small, are clear and in focus. But when it comes to the figure in blue, the lenses fail me. I can only see that it is a young man, not very tall, with a darkish complexion and thick black hair. I can make out nothing of his face, partly because he is moving incessantly, his back turned to me most of the time as he faces the wood pile.

I take a walk, and I find the pile of logs. Although I didn't recognize its location, it's a place I pass every time I go to visit the Parkers. The road is a little wider at this point and the wood is piled up along its outer rim, where it can easily be picked up by the logging trucks.

I am surprised by the size of the wood pile. It's almost as high as I am and maybe fifteen meters long. The logs, all of the same length, have been placed with such care that their round cut surfaces are perfectly aligned, although the pile as a whole is curved, following the curve of the road. It's beautiful to look at.

The next day as I'm sitting on the terrace, a voice calls out to me. I have a visitor. It's Elio, approaching from the side of the *stallina*, naked to the waist. He's come to say something. It spills out so quickly that I have to reconstruct what he said. He's begun to stack up wood under our oak tree. He would have asked my permission, but I wasn't there at the time. Costanzo told him to go ahead and begin stacking it; he said I wouldn't mind.

"That's fine, that's fine," I say. I don't want to admit that in my preoccupation with the wood pile on the next hill, I never noticed the one right under my nose. "Would you like to come inside?"

"I'm indecent," Elio protests, putting his hands over his nipples as he accepts my invitation and steps into the kitchen. By contrast with his dark drinker's complexion, his bare chest is starkly white. His chest seems in some way more distinctive, more individual than his face.

"How have you been?" I ask him.

"*Mah,*" he shrugs. "Not bad. I hurt my finger"— he holds out his left hand of which the index finger is crooked—"sawing wood."

"Did you break it? Didn't you go to the hospital?"

"No, no, it wasn't broken, but all the tendons... I went to the hospital, but only after nine days, and they couldn't..." His sentences trail off. He has something else on his mind.

"I saw you the other day," he blurts out, "at the Co-op, but you didn't recognize me."

I smile blankly, slow to comprehend.

"I was there with Paola," Elio persists plaintively. "I made a sign, but you didn't see us."

There is a childlike, wounded outrage in his tone. The implication is clear: I didn't want to acknowledge the two of them in public.

"When was that?" I attempt to retreat behind a faulty memory. In reality, I am sometimes so distracted that it's entirely possible I looked straight at them without recognizing them. But I feel annoyed by his accusation. Even his naked chest now seems like an affront.

Suddenly Elio makes a motion for me to be silent. His face changes. He seems to be listening. A little smile appears, then he says, "I have to go. He doesn't know the path; he's taking it for the first time."

Confused, I follow him out onto the terrace and around the side of the house to the front. And there they are, the mules and the mule driver, suddenly life-size with his red skull-cap, grinning curiously.

Standing next to him—of course, I should have known: the figure in blue, the creator of the beautiful wood pile, is Flavio.

The mules are huge. There are six of them and one horse—the horse is much smaller—crowding together under the shade of the oak tree. They stand quietly, swishing their tails. A tiny bell tinkles from one of their harnesses. I feel overwhelmed by their hugeness and closeness.

The mule driver exchanges some words with Elio: directions to a watering-place. Then, waving a greeting, he mounts the horse and starts to move away slowly.

The mules, tied together, turn and fall into place one by one, proceeding single file up the hill.

I'm hanging up my laundry when something falls with a loud smack from the roof to the ground directly in front of me. It's a snake, all coiled up. To my surprise, instead of slithering away, it stays like that. At first I can't see where its head is; then, as I look more closely, there seem to be two tails, and the head is a wide-open mouth holding what looks like a black frog. The coil remains nearly immobile, only twitching slightly, as if it had reached an impasse. I pick up a stone and throw it. The snake is gone in a flash, releasing its prey, which turns out to be a lizard and runs up the wall of the house, apparently unharmed.

All the time, beneath the peaceful appearance of the landscape, dramas like this are being enacted.

Over at La Croce, so idyllic in the morning sun, there in the big house is Flavio, about to start his new job on the highway crew, perhaps dreading it as a fate worse than death. Costanzo told me that Flavio prefers winter to summer and night-time to day. He said it with a little smile as if to say, what a strange bird.

I realize that I don't know what the lives of the people here are really like. I have no idea of their difficulties, any more than they have of mine.

For some reason this reminds me of the Fattore, the man who used to manage the estate when it still belonged to the Marchese, his responsibilities becoming progressively diminished as the farmhouses were sold off one by one to foreigners. He had a mustache and always struck me as a dignified man. In his last weeks, he suffered from *Fuoco di Sant'Antonio,* or shingles. He walked around with dark glasses and a straw hat on his head. One morning, he sent his wife to the market for some fish. He had a dentist's appointment that afternoon and told her he wanted "something soft to eat." When she returned he was dead. He had hanged himself.

Whenever I used to see him, my only thought was, "A dignified man."

25

The hunting season has begun. Hunters have been driving up by the house, three, four, and five of them crammed into a jeep or some small Fiat. Then I hear shots popping up in the woods. In the old days, the right to hunt was a privilege of the nobility; now it is a popular sport. The men look at once ridiculous and frightening in their camouflage outfits.

Early on a Sunday morning, I happen to be looking out the window and see Renato, Lorenzo, Marcello, and Marcello's son walking by the house with their guns and dogs, all got up in camouflage. Marcello orders his dog to go "this way;" it runs off in the opposite direction.

Several hours later, Renato comes by again alone, this time without his dog. "Any success?" I ask him, leaning out the window. *Niente*—not even a hare. He walks on forlornly across the field, looking right and left, as if hoping against hope that something will poke its head out of the ground.

I've heard that Lorenzo sometimes takes part in the squads of thirty to forty men who hunt wild boar up in the woods. Starting from the bottom, they spread out and make noise to chase the boar uphill, tiring them out. And at the top, the men with the best aim are waiting.

The Parkers tell me that the hunters are not supposed to shoot at night, but some of them stay in the hills until after dark and then drive back down past Castellina, stopping at the field below and shining their spotlights into it. If there are any *caprioli*, they are blinded by the lights and freeze. The men shoot them and then quickly, in a matter of minutes, toss the carcasses onto plastic sheets, wrap them up, throw them into the trunk and are gone.

When Richard and Libby hear hunters coming, they lean out the windows and shout to give the *caprioli* warning. But sometimes they're too late, and the next morning they'll find a leg or some other piece left behind.

I call Libby on the phone. "Have you heard the latest about Ziegmann?" she asks me. "Well, listen to this. Sabina says he spray-painted a red man on her garden wall! Of course she can't know it was him. She called the *vigili*. They laughed when they saw it. I find it hard to believe myself. I mean, he's a professor, isn't he? Even if he is a bit round the bend. It could have been vandals... But she's absolutely certain it was Claudio. Poor Sabina! She sounded absolutely distraught. You know she can't laugh about anything. She was so upset she had to leave again for Germany right away. Still, she probably started the whole thing by not letting him plant his tomatoes where he's always done."

I ask Libby if she's seen the "red man" herself. Is it a stick figure? Is it obscene?

"No, I didn't see it, unfortunately. I couldn't get anything out of Sabina, and the *vigili* helped her clean it off, so we can only speculate. I asked Renato, and he admitted it was vulgar. But, of course, I don't know if his idea of vulgar is the same as mine. While they were at it, the *vigili* said that the wall itself was illegal, and so were some of the other modifications they've both made to their houses. Claudio's going to be sorry for this one. Anyway, I think we're going to have to write him off. We won't invite him anymore. Don't you agree?"

I'm calling to invite the Parkers for dinner at Querceto. But Libby asks if we can postpone it. She says Richard has been in a bad mood lately; he's started laying the parquet floor in the studio and it's a disaster. When they bought the wood twelve years ago, they only opened one of the boxes. Now it turns out that perhaps a third of them are unusable. The boards are crooked.

I say that's fine, we'll do it another time.

Up in the woods where I take my walks, cardboard signs have appeared tacked to several trees: *From 25.9. to 10.11. it is Forbidden to Enter the Chestnut Grove.*

The chestnut season, too, has arrived.

Silvana laughs when I ask her about the signs. "Those are Elio's. He puts those up." Apparently his *marroneta* is at the edge of the woods, so he is worried about trespassers. What I think of as "the woods," wild territory belonging to no one, is in fact crisscrossed with invisible lines of demarcation. Everyone has their own little piece.

When I first saw Elio's signs, I was intimidated and turned back. But after speaking to Silvana, I venture a little ways in, past two Fiat Pandas parked just past the biggest sign, until I can hear low voices in the woods above me. I don't recognize the voices.

The chestnuts are thick on the ground. I pick up one of the green prickly round things that are lying everywhere, almost the size and color of tennis balls; I try stepping on it. It's all a soft white pulp inside. It's the brown ones that have dried out and cracked open that are good. If you step down on those lightly with your heel, the rich dark chestnuts slip out. In some cases they've already burst out of their shells and are lying naked amidst the dry leaves on the ground. I quickly stuff a few into my pockets. Sometimes there are four to a pod, sometimes three.

All the while I continue to hear muffled voices through the trees, of people close by yet invisible. It's a peculiar sound, an intimate murmuring, like interference on a telephone line. I think of that story about Lodovico and his brother's wife. I try to imagine how it could have happened.

The Donatis are spending every day now up in the woods. Enrico has taken a two-week vacation to help with the chestnuts. The first five days he spent cleaning the *marroneta* in preparation for harvest, removing all the brush with a hand-held power saw. Elio does not clean his part, and it still looks like ordinary woods. But the Donatis transform theirs into a beautiful light grove, where the chestnuts drop onto the soft, springy ground.

"You should come see us up there," Silvana tells me. She says this is her favorite time of year, and she prefers being in the woods to being at La Croce.

"It's not a dark, hidden place. It's lovely, when the sun shines it stays light until eight."

Of course, the day I've chosen to go and "help" the Donatis with the chestnuts, it's drizzling. I set out at about ten in the morning with my umbrella. As I approach the little cabin, I see Enrico sitting inside the door and Silvana off to the right, making her way up the slope followed by Sama. She is wearing thick woolen socks and hiking shoes, and several cardigans one on top of the other. She has an umbrella with different-colored segments and a basket over her arm. I call out to her.

"Go into the cabin. I'll join you in a minute."

I don't see Costanzo. I wave hello to Enrico and follow Silvana, saying I'll help her. She laughs and protests that it's raining too much. But she seems happy when I insist and start gathering up chestnuts at a little distance from her.

"Just a few more and then we'll stop."

I quickly become infected with the compulsion to pick up just a few more, and a few more. In some places, Enrico has built little fences to prevent the chestnuts from rolling down the hill.

"Let's just look and see if there are any mushrooms," Silvana says, "with this rain." She jokes: "One mushroom, and then we'll stop." Enrico has begun calling out to us to come back to the cabin.

"Yes, we're coming!" And we move on further up the hill. Finally, as the rain is turning into a downpour, we have no choice but to stop.

It's the first time I've been inside the cabin. Although it's no more than a few meters squared, the tiny space contains a real wood stove, a table, two chairs, and a shelf with cooking supplies.

"This is our other house—you've never seen it? Do you like it? And this is our sofa," Silvana indicates a tree stump in the corner. "Please have a seat. Make yourself comfortable." I've never seen her this high-spirited, laughing at my astonished face and at herself.

On the shelf are dishes, pots, wine, oil, and seasonings; a bag of pasta and a few little jars of homemade sauce. There is a whole chicken cooking on the stove. Some co-workers of Enrico's are expected for lunch later.

Enrico is sitting at the table sorting the chestnuts which he has gathered in old paint cans. The bad ones are for rabbit food, the good are filled into burlap sacks to be collected by the buyer who comes round to all the farms. They get two thousand five hundred lire a kilo, while on the market, the chestnuts will sell for between six and eight thousand lire.

I sense that Enrico doesn't like my presence here. Probably he is worried I might stay for lunch. I try to make conversation with him, extracting facts and figures. This has been a bad year because of the drought in the summer months. They will gather perhaps fifteen *quintali* in all. Last year was a good year; they gathered thirty-five. A *quintale* is a hundred kilos. One person can collect about fifty kilos a day. But with Costanzo not helping...

"Where is Costanzo?" I've been expecting him to show up any minute with a bucketful of chestnuts.

It turns out that after the first day, he refused to come along, saying his legs hurt him. I am shocked by this news. I can't tell if Silvana thinks he is malingering and is angry with him.

When I say I have to go, Silvana produces a bottle of orangeade and a chunk of cake. Enrico loosens up, relieved that I'm not going to stay longer, and we all have a little snack, standing around the table.

Silvana said that Costanzo doesn't even want to walk as far as the loggia anymore. I didn't know what she meant by "loggia" at the time, but didn't bother to ask. Now I think I know. There's an odd little structure halfway between Querceto and La Croce, off to the side of the road. I wonder how long it's been there without my having noticed it. It's so bizarre-looking that I am almost embarrassed to examine it. I make sure I'm alone before stepping off the path to take a look.

It's a sort of tiny hut made of wire mesh on a wooden frame, open on one side, with a few boards on top for a roof. There's just enough room in this little shelter for two old car seats positioned side by side, looking into the valley. Costanzo must have hammered the thing together. I try to picture the two of them, walking the several hundred meters from La Croce to sit here and gaze at a view that differs by a few degrees from the view they have at their own house. I can imagine that Silvana would enjoy the make-believe of calling this construction a *loggia*, reclining in the car seat as if it were a beach chair in a comfortable vacation spot. After all, we foreigners who come here do nothing but talk about the view and sit around looking into the distance.

Perhaps, in order to imagine for himself a retirement of ease, Costanzo found that what he wanted was *a different place*. But unlike Silvana, he would not be able to believe in the fantasy. Looking at what he had made, he would see clearly that it is a cage.

It's been getting cold at night. I've checked all the storage spaces at Querceto and come up with more warm blankets and a small electrical heater. There are two dusty hot-water bottles hanging from a hook in the upstairs hallway, which haven't been used in ages. One is cracked, but the other seems in good shape, and I've washed it out. If I'm desperate, I might even try the old contraption we once found at a flea market in Florence, a clay pot that can be filled with hot coals, suspended in a light wooden frame. We were told that this bed warmer is colloquially known as a *prete*, a "priest."

There is of course the fireplace, and the wood stove in the kitchen. But I'll have to cut some more logs.

26

There has been a *disgrazia* at La Croce. Flavio has had an accident. It was only his third day on the new job. He was walking behind one of the men with grass-cutting machines. The machine tossed up a big rock that hit him in the jaw, breaking all of his front teeth. Luckily it didn't hit him a little higher, Silvana says, or he would be dead.

He was taken to the hospital at Careggi, where they extracted the roots of his teeth and the broken fragments of bone from his jaw. He can't speak or eat, only drink milk in little sips. He is in terrible pain. And instead of keeping him in the hospital, Silvana tells me indignantly, where at least they could monitor his healing and feed him intravenously, they sent him right home.

"They don't want to pay anything, that's what it is."

The *Comune* of Borgo, his employer, will pay for dentures, but he will never be the same, and they will certainly give him the cheapest, most unbecoming and impractical kind.

I think about Flavio lying there in that dark house, his jaw covered with bandages. I feel that his suffering is somehow doubly mute: not only that he can't speak but that, because of the way he is, he can't make clear to himself the pain of his existence.

On my way back from a walk in the woods, I come upon Elio standing by some small piles of logs. He is looking down the hill after a truck that must have just been to pick some of them up. In his left hand he clutches a large hook-shaped knife, with a hand-beaten blade two inches wide. He seems in a daze.

I greet him and ask about Flavio. He says he is a little better, not in as much pain anymore, but he can still only take liquid food. "It's a terrible blow. But," pointing up at the sky, "one has to accept whatever the Lord gives." Waving his lethal-looking weapon, he adds that it's hard because Flavio is *un bravo ragazzo*. Yes, I agree, he's a good kid. I feel convinced at this moment that Elio doesn't care about him at all.

Elio is looking at me expectantly and I wonder what else I should say. Then I realize he is merely waiting for me to move on. I say goodbye and start walking down the hill. When I look back over my shoulder, I see him bend over his wood pile, apparently searching for something hidden among the logs.

Two airplanes pass overhead at the same time, making the sky resonate as if it were made of a thin sheet of metal.

On my next outing to Florence, I buy a *torta della nonna* for the Donatis at my favorite bakery. I also want to find some little gift specially for Flavio, something that will help him while away the hours. I decide to pick up a comic book. If he can't read, he can still follow the story of the pictures. And even if he can read, it shouldn't be taken as an insult since one still quite often sees adults reading comic books on the train.

The large kiosk in the center of the station has everything: newspapers, magazines, even do-it-yourself manuals for plumbing and wiring. A man in front of me gives the vendor some money and the vendor in return hands him a little stack of pornographic cards. He flips through them until he finds one he likes, then he walks away swiftly, looking at it. Another man is crowding me from behind. He is beginning to make me nervous, until I realize I'm blocking his view of a magazine. The magazine is sealed in plastic; one of its titles promises: "I will take off my bathing suit under water." Embarrassed, I step aside to let the man make his purchase.

I settle on a comic book entitled *The Wolves of*

Colorado.

As I approach La Croce, greeted as always by Sama, I am surprised to see Flavio sitting out in front with Costanzo. He looks fairly normal, only a little puffy around the mouth, with a black line of stitches on his lip.

I have the comic book in my hand, so I give it to him straight off. He seems at first nonplussed, then amused. He nods vigorously: "I used to buy these, yes, I'll read this, thank you." He puts his hand in front of his mouth as he speaks to hide the lack of his front teeth.

Costanzo takes the book from him and looks at it dubiously: "You like this stuff?"

Flavio laughs, still concealing his mouth, and looks at me: "Yes, yes, it's good. Colorado, that's a place in America, isn't it?"

"Yes, but I've never been there." I suddenly feel this gift was a mistake after all: I've underestimated Flavio's intelligence. "It has high mountains," I add factually, to cover my embarrassment. "How are you?"

Flavio shrugs, grinning sheepishly. Costanzo says: "Bad, he's bad. He can't eat."

Flavio explains the incident again to me, never taking the hand away from his mouth. There was a sort of tractor for cutting grass, not only down on the ground but also higher up, on roadside embankments. He was walking not behind the tractor, as Silvana said, but in front of it. Nobody had told him that you weren't supposed to walk in front of the tractor, and anyway he was far away from it, a good twenty meters away, and he had just turned around when the rock came flying and hit him.

We go inside. Silvana murmurs something to Flavio, who bolts off toward his house. A few minutes later, a frenzied outburst from Sama is followed by a shuffling at the door. A female voice calls out: *Permesso?*

"Oh, Paola, come in! Come in!"

I can tell from Silvana's show of surprise and delight that Flavio's mother has been summoned. A skeletally thin woman, she enters the room deferentially, her arms folded closely about her, smiling and nodding. She sits down on the edge of a chair. She has evidently come both to help eat the cake and to acknowledge the gift to Flavio, which has given my visit a somewhat official character. She smiles at me in a forbearing way which makes me think I have probably insulted her more than once by not recognizing her in Vigliano.

"ANAS is going to pay a million eight," she says when I ask about compensation. "The dentist said it could cost eight million to have his teeth replaced."

She says it so calmly that I can't help exclaiming: "But that's terrible! Doesn't it make you very angry?"

"Of course, one is angry, but what can one do? You can't go and hit them with a big stick, even if that's what you'd like to do. Anyway," she adds with a little laugh, "then you'd go from being in the right to being in the wrong, wouldn't you?"

Behind Paola's soft-spoken manner I sense a certain strength, as of someone who will bend but not break.

"He's only thirty-three, you know," she adds politely. "He's young. He should have a good set of teeth, not any old ones. And he's also lost the feeling on that side of his lip."

Silvana murmurs something about *disgrazia*.

We are all silent for a moment. All at once, Paola leans forward and touches my knee as if on an impulse she can contain no longer.

"So—children?" she asks, smiling. "Nothing yet? A husband?"

I smile back. "Not even a *fidanzato*." I suddenly dislike her and notice the mustache hairs on her upper lip. "I'm fine the way I am."

"That's what Flavio says, too." She sighs. "He says he's fine the way he is."

27

I am walking down the hill toward Casabassa, slipping and sliding with each step on the loose stones, when I notice a man standing inside the gates, looking expectantly in my direction. It is not Wenzel. The gates are open, and to the left I see a little faded red truck. When I come closer, the man smiles and holds out his hand.

"Squilloni Antonio. Pleased to meet you."

He is bald, with a florid complexion and three teeth standing staunchly and individually in their gum-sockets. He immediately launches into a torrent of words, from which I glean that he works as a caretaker for several of the German houses in the area. He has recently started working for *il dottore*. He fumes: "Renato is a trouble-maker...."

I don't understand what his beef with Renato is. I wonder if his showing up is the result of my letter to Wenzel, though in it I didn't blame Renato at all.

Squilloni shakes his finger at me. "Renato is not a sincere person. And I'm not saying it just because he's not here. I would say it to his face. I don't say things about people that I wouldn't tell them to their face."

In fact he is speaking so loudly that if Renato were anywhere in the vicinity, he could certainly hear him. He goes on in this vein, calling Renato "a fox." Little drops of saliva fly from his mouth and one actually hits me in the face.

Il dottore phoned him the day before, he says, to ask if his cisterns were filling up. And he has reason to be anxious, because last year he traveled all the way down from Germany on a Saturday only to find out that he had no water, and was forced to return on Sunday.

I reply somewhat coldly that I am familiar with this situation. All along I've thought of Wenzel as sharing my interests; now it occurs to me that we could just as easily be in competition. Oddly, Squilloni doesn't seem to be aware of Adriani's attachment.

"With several houses attached to the same spring," I say, "it's important that all of us share the water amicably."

Squilloni eagerly agrees. "Everyone should sit down at a table and talk together." He goes so far as to suggest the use of his own house as a neutral place – "the house of no one" – for the presumptive meeting to take place. This seems bizarre, coming from a man I met only a few minutes ago. I find myself increasingly disliking him, perhaps just because he talks so much.

He rants on and on, complaining about his taxes and contrasting his fate to that of a rich industrialist who committed suicide after being caught in a political scandal. "This man said that he'd had a thousand desires in his life, and that he had been able to realize almost all of them. Now I, what do I have? Of my desires, I haven't realized a single one. And yet I do not have to go and kill myself today. But it would be better if everyone could realize a hundred desires."

There is something debased in his manner, which probably comes from having worked for foreigners for so long. Under the veneer of servile affability is a tangle of envy and righteousness. He has made a living by playing the role he feels is expected of him: the salt-of-the-earth Tuscan. At the end he says: "If you want to come to my house to wash when you have no water, you are welcome."

Another rainy, foggy day. And it's cold. I make a fire in the kitchen at ten and keep it going throughout the day. I sit as close to it as I can, wrapped in a blanket.

In the afternoon Renato and Lorenzo come by the house, Lorenzo riding atop the John Deere, Renato following after on a rickety-looking antique. I see

Renato stop and motion to Lorenzo to go on ahead without him. I go and open the door.

"Oh, *ciao*, how are things?" he greets me exuberantly.

"You're going to have water problems," he announces then without further preliminary. "The German from Casabassa is having big water tanks put in. Three of them, that hold thirty thousand liters each. That's ninety thousand liters altogether. *Porca miseria*, do you know how long it will take for those to fill up? It will take a month, and until then, nothing will come to Querceto."

I am slow to comprehend. He senses that I'm not reacting properly. His show of indignation increases. "It isn't right! If I had my cows at Casabassa, I wouldn't have a drop of water for them. Fortunately, they're up in the hills now. But what about you? Squilloni's the one who is going to install the tanks. Then you'll have to ask him to turn the water off so that you can have some. This will be a big problem—for you more than for me. If the *tedesco* is going to be that way, then you'll just have no choice but to put in a divider, so he gets his part, you get yours, I get mine, and that's that."

The thought of our shut-off valve crosses my mind, but I keep it to myself. I say that I'll try to speak to Wenzel about it.

"But I didn't say anything! You didn't hear anything from me!" Renato holds his palms up. His manner changes as abruptly as it did before. He says goodbye cheerfully.

That explains Squilloni. His sudden appearance at Casabassa, the pre-emptive attack against Renato. If you wait long enough, things fall into place. Is Renato really as outraged as he pretends, or is he just using this as an opportunity to turn the tables, divert attention from Adriani's tap?

I can't take anything at face value. Perhaps he wants to pit me against Wenzel. Perhaps our talk about contracts has Renato worried, he envisions a league of foreigners against him. It could be a frightening prospect from his point of view, the *tedeschi* ganging up on him with their seemingly unlimited supply of money. He has no idea how little likelihood of this there is.

In the evening I go to visit Costanzo and Silvana. It's still raining and particularly dark, and I walk quickly with my umbrella and my little flashlight. When I get to La Croce it seems strange that everything is so dark and silent. It isn't even nine o'clock. There is no Sama to bark at me as I approach their house; the front door is closed. I knock. I hear their voices from deep inside, wondering who it could be. I call out, saying it's me. I hear Costanzo begin to chuckle as he comes to open the door. "Cristina, come in!"

Silvana marvels at how cold my face is when she kisses me. "Like in the winter!"

They have a nice little fire going. Costanzo keeps on chuckling for a bit after we've sat down. "You did well to come," he says several times.

It turns out that even their "own" Germans, Maia and Manfredo, have taken to going over to Renato's in the evening, deserting them.

"You don't go to Renato's?" I ask tentatively.

"No, no, we don't go." They both shake their heads and I don't press it further.

I ask them how Flavio is doing, because I haven't seen him in a while. And now here is a piece of good news: Flavio has started working for Renato. Apparently he gets along well with Lorenzo; the two of them share a passion for cruising the hills on their mopeds. It's only an informal thing, to bridge the time until he goes back to his job on the *autostrada*.

"But who knows," Silvana says. "Perhaps he won't have to go back at all anymore."

If that were true, I could forgive Renato anything.

28

Once again, the water has stopped coming to Querceto. The cisterns, empty. This is craziness, when all around the pipes are running full and plenty. What is it this time? Another clogged tube? Adriani's faucet, when I checked it, was turned off.

I've called Landi to bring me more water, but he can't come until tomorrow. Generini is coming the day after to look into the problem. Meanwhile, Libby and Richard have invited me to spend the night in their guest room. I am abandoning Querceto for their comfortable, warm castle, where there are wood stoves in every room and Richard keeps fires going from his never-ending supply of perfectly sized logs.

"It's no use worrying about it today," Libby tells me.

In the late afternoon, Libby and I take a walk from Castellina back to Querceto because I've forgotten to bring my toothbrush. The weather is crisp and beautiful. We take the upper path through the woods, past the Donatis' little hut, which is all closed up again. The chestnut season is over. The leaves are turning yellow and orange; the ground is covered with prickly hulls, and there are still quite a few chestnuts left lying there. Most are soft or have wormholes, but we find some good ones and take them with us.

The sun is already setting when we come out of the woods, and the sky is glowing softly. Libby points out the field below Casabassa, which is a bright, poisonous light-green, with grass so young and tender it looks like fuzz.

"Look how beautiful," she says. "I wish I could paint that."

She tells me Richard is still working on the parquet floor. He won't know until the end if he has enough boards to make it work.

At dinner they both seem distracted, irritated with each other. I sense that I am in the way, an obstacle to some currents passing between them. I pretend not to notice anything amiss and try to lighten the mood by telling amusing stories. But they fall flat; they sound boring even to me. Each time there is a gap in the conversation, my heart sinks.

I am glad when I can retreat to my little guest room. It's luxurious compared to Querceto, with a double bed and patterned comforter. I look inside the wardrobe: it's empty but for a few precisely folded towels. The doors open and shut smoothly with a rich solid feeling. There are moments when there can be no greater consolation than a little room with a made bed and a wardrobe whose only purpose is to contain its own spicy fragrance of wood.

I look out the small window at the black, protective hulk of the mountain. To the right of it I can see lights down in the valley. Querceto is somewhere on the other side, in darkness.

I know that the time has come for me to leave, regardless of what happens with the water. I can't manage the winter at Querceto. The little electrical heater and the wood stove are no match for the damp cold. I have to book my flight.

The next morning, I am back at Querceto just in time to see Landi arriving on this tractor, pulling the water tank. We smirk at each other with *déjà vu*, exchange a few words about the cold.

After he has filled the water in, for some reason the pump doesn't start up. He yanks the lid off the electrical box, sending a screw flying irretrievably into some dark corner of the *stallina*. He jabs at the electric connections with the plastic lid, causing sparks. The pump starts up; then dies again. Without a word, he goes back to his tractor and returns with a dented tin of electrolyte grease, which he proceeds to slather in big messy gobs all over the connections. After a bit more trial and error, the pump starts up again.

"Go into the kitchen and turn on the water."

I obediently go, and come back out.

"Now turn it off."

I hurry back.

"Now on! Now off!" He has me running back and forth, a big grin on his face.

Once more: *Apra! Chiuda!*

Finally he replaces the lid (without the screw) on the box; wipes his grease spatula on the water tube.

"Any more problems, call me."

I pay him for the water, ask how much I owe for the "repair." He replies, magnanimously: *Niente*.

Later in the afternoon Renato comes driving up the hill. I watch him park his car and get out, looking around nervously. I don't go downstairs. I don't want to talk to him.

He calls out: "Hey! Anybody home?"

I relent and open the door.

And then it all comes out. Landi told him that I didn't have water, and he got worried. He set about investigating the matter on his own. What he found out is unbelievable. He obviously thinks I won't believe him. But it's so crazy that it must be true.

Renato had also complained to Ziegmann about Wenzel's planned mega-cisterns, and Ziegmann saw his chance to show where his allegiance lay. Thinking he was doing Renato a favor, he cut the tube above the field where Renato sometimes grazes his cows. That same field that Libby and I were admiring on our walk, with its fresh, bright young grass! He told Renato proudly about his act of sabotage.

I start laughing. The more I try to imagine it, the more it makes me laugh.

"I had nothing to do with this," Renato protests uncertainly. "I didn't know about it until he told me this morning."

No doubt he feels his credibility is shaky.

"I told him it was wrong. The *professore* is a little—" He taps his forefinger to his head.

"I know. I heard about the red man."

"Don't worry, I've patched it up. The water should be coming now. And it won't happen again."

I don't know which of us is more relieved. We talk for a while after this. He brings up Wenzel's tanks again.

"Perhaps they're not such a bad idea," I say. "They can fill up in the winter months, when there is plenty of water, and serve as a reservoir in the summer. Perhaps we should put some in at Querceto, too. Then we all won't have to worry so much."

I have the impression Renato is disappointed by my conciliatory attitude.

With all this, I've forgotten to call Generini and tell him there is no need to come. Yet I'm glad to see him. In a strange way, although I've only met him once before, he seems like an old friend. This time he comes in a little van and is dressed more appropriately for outdoor work.

Perhaps he was looking forward to going the whole length of the tube on foot. Instead we merely stand on the terrace and talk. He accepts half a glass of orangeade. I tell him about Ziegmann, and admit that I haven't taken any action about Adriani's attachment.

"I can't get everyone to agree on what to do."

Generini merely smiles, as if this didn't surprise him in the slightest. "It's always wise not to make enemies."

I wonder if he's just humoring me. This was certainly not Fabbri's or Pieri's view of things.

"The problem of water in this region," he says

then, "is like water itself. You can't grasp it. Every time you think you have found the solution, it runs out of your hands."

He could leave right away, but we stand on the terrace together for about half an hour. He remarks on the view. "It's nice up here." He is from across the hills over there, near Marradi. Still part of the municipality of Borgo, but in the Romagna, very different from Tuscany. We talk about the houses that are high up in those distant bluish hills, reachable only by mule paths. Although we are talking about nothing much, I feel that our conversation is characterized by an extreme delicacy, like a piece played *pianissimo* on the piano. In the silences between our remarks there is a consciousness of distance, as if our attempt at communication were a fragile spider's thread connecting two worlds very far apart.

At the end he gives me an odd handshake, holding out his left hand to my right as he turns away, in a fleeting sideward touch.

It has long gotten too cold to eat my supper on the terrace. But at night, before locking up the house, I go out and stand for a few minutes, looking into the valley. The houses and villages are hazy lights, some single, some clustered together. Here and there I can follow the headlights of a car threading its way through the darkness. I hear dogs barking and sometimes, very faintly, the sound of music and laughter—like from those gatherings there used to be at La Croce in the old days, when Amedeo was alive and played the accordion. The sound seems small and forlorn, vainly trying to assert itself against the deep and silent sky.

All of this gives me a thumb-sized pain in my chest, a mixture of exhilaration and longing. I feel the dark landscape around me, the infinite things in it that I can't see or know. And the world seems filled to overflowing with the warmth and goodness of strangers.

29

The last days are spent packing up, tidying and cleaning the house, and saying goodbye to the Donatis and the Parkers. Richard has given me little petroleum cubes that make lighting fires easier; all this time, like a fool, I've been struggling with damp newspaper.

"You can always come and stay in our guest room," they tell me, holding back the second part of the thought – "if Querceto is really going to be sold."

Now that I have so few days left, they seem to pass even more quickly. Sitting in Costanzo and Silvana's kitchen, I find myself looking attentively at the light green oilcloth on the table, with its floral design in red and white and its crocheted yarn border, trying to imprint it on my memory. But I know that I won't remember it. In a few weeks or even less time, I won't be able to visualize it in my mind.

Costanzo says, "You'll write to us now and then, won't you? Send us a card." And this takes me by surprise, it makes me happy, because all these years I've never known if my Christmas greetings were received or read by them.

On my last evening I walk over to La Croce to say goodbye again to Costanzo and Silvana. But it's a sad goodbye because Costanzo is upstairs in bed; he has fallen ill again. This time it was something different, Silvana explains—*non poteva fare la pipì*. They took him to the hospital in Borgo, where he was catheterized. If he's not better in a month, he might need an operation. "It would be a disaster," she says. "They would have to do it in Florence because they don't have the necessary apparatus in Borgo."

I think it might be best to leave again right away. But she presses me to stay, "just a little bit." Even though Costanzo can't come downstairs right now, she says, he would want me to stay too. "He can hear what we're saying."

Despite Costanzo's illness there is a lightness in our conversation. Silvana wants to know about the food I'll eat when I get back to America. I say it's more or less the same as here, nothing strange, not horse or donkey meat like up in Mantua, or fried frogs, or dogs like they eat in China.

She laughs. But horse meat, she says, is supposed to be good for people who are anemic. And they eat frogs here in Tuscany too, at the Festa dell'Unità in Borgo. Though she doesn't like them much either.

Silvana asks me how many hours it will take me to get back home. Do I like going on airplanes?

"Very much. It's nice to be able to look down at the clouds, and the mountains, and the ocean."

She marvels; she's heard this said before. "Above the clouds it's always sunny?"

Nonetheless she would prefer to go on a ship, like the one Salvatore is always talking about, that he and Marietta take to Sardinia. *A village on the move.* "And underneath they put the cars and even entire trains. I wonder how all that can stay afloat?"

She says it looking at me expectantly, as if I might know the answer. I try to remember my physics lessons, but all that comes to me is a phrase, "the volume of water displaced." I look back at her helplessly. I don't know. It does seem that the ship should sink.

"You've never been on a ship then, only on airplanes? Salvatore always talks about the ship. One day, I wouldn't mind going on one myself."

"Why not? After Costanzo gets better, I mean. Enrico could look after the animals, and you and Costanzo could take the ship to visit Salvatore and Marietta in Sardinia."

Even as I say this, I know it will never happen.

When it's time for me to leave, Silvana calls upstairs to Costanzo to say goodbye to me, and he shouts from his bed, in the same voice as if he were shouting across a field, with the same slow forming of the sounds to give them time to carry, "*Ciao figliola!*"

I shout back, "Get better," and "good night."

Silvana puts on the little light above the door for me. I turn on my flashlight. It seems colder than before. Silvana hugs me a second time, saying, "Let's hope," and "One never knows, does one, whether one will see each other again."

I remember our goodbyes from other years; she has always said things like this. I suddenly realize what it is that we foreigners mean to her: our coming and going, like that of seasonal birds, is a measure of time passing.

As I go up the slope from their house I turn back again and again to wave and say *ciao*. Silvana too says *ciao* again and again, at shorter intervals than I'm saying it, so that there is a sort of syncopation between us. Her voice seems to get lower and lower and the last vowel is drawn out longer into a deep *oo* sound, until her calls scarcely resemble a human word anymore.

I turn my flashlight off again. The night is very dark; there are no stars or moon to be seen through the clouds.

But the air feels fresh and nice, with a softness to it as if there could be snow.

III. *Two Years Later*

Sic fluit occulte, sic multos decipit aetas
Sic venit ad finem quidquid in orbe manet
Heu heu praeteritum non est revocabile tempus
Heu propius tacito mors venit ipsa pede

Thus time flows secretly, deceiving many;
Thus everything in the world comes to an end.
Alas, alas!—the time gone by cannot be brought back.
Alas!—death approaches with silent steps.

Angelo Poliziano
(On the clock in Santa Maria Novella)

30

Seeing Silvana the first time is terrible. I've stopped at La Croce on my way up from the train station, even before going to Querceto. As I get out of the car I see her approach from her vegetable garden. She is walking slowly, with her eyes lowered, not looking at me. When she reaches me, she clutches me and presses her face tightly against my neck. I hug her back, but at this moment I feel nothing but embarrassment. Tears streaming out of her eyes, she says, "My life is finished." Then she takes my hand and we walk to her front door. I am aware of fighting back an impulse to smile stupidly, and of my complete inability to grasp Costanzo's death.

She asks me in, makes the usual remark about my sitting on the fireplace bench, but only half-heartedly. She gestures around the kitchen. "Right? The house is empty, all empty. Costanzo was always so happy when you arrived."

She tells me about his illness. He was in the hospital for an entire month. He didn't want to be left alone, so she and Enrico stayed with him day and night, taking turns. The operation went well, but afterward, turning over one day in his too narrow hospital bed, he fell out and broke a rib. She was by his side when it happened, but she couldn't stop it. "He was too unlucky."

It was the beginning of the end. After that he got worse and worse. The prostate cancer had spread to other places. Gradually the rest of his system gave up.

"He wouldn't eat anything. The hospital food he certainly wouldn't touch at all. The nurses said to me, why don't you eat it? And so I did. We brought homemade food for him instead: thick, nourishing soups made with fresh meat broth. But he hardly ate any of that either. He ate nothing. Of course they gave him nutriments intravenously. But what he needed was real, good food: and he couldn't eat it."

Silvana disappears briefly into the back room; she wants to show me the thermos container they used to carry the soup. She takes off the outer lid and the screw cap and shows me the empty interior of the thermos.

31

I sit on the terrace at Querceto. The sky is cloudy, there is a steady breeze, and every once in a while thunder rolls in the distance; but the air feels mild. There are still a few irises by the front door, but for the most part I think they are finished. The broom is in full blossom and there are all kinds of wildflowers near the house— poppies, buttercups, and daisies. The grass on our field has not been mowed yet. The wind blowing through it makes ripples and waves as if it were water.

In a few days I will hand over the keys to the buyers, Alberto and Anna. Alberto is Domenico's brother. They live in Bologna and will be able to come in the summers and throughout the year. I felt an immediate liking for them; I can't think of anyone I'd rather give the house to. They have two beautiful daughters: Elsa and Viola.

The house will be lived in again. That makes me happy.

In coming to terms with the necessity of selling Querceto, I've often thought about Ziegmann's statement that we don't own anything here, we are just temporary custodians. I think about how many people have lived in Querceto before us; how often it happened over the years that people would tell us that they, or an aunt or a cousin, had been born in this house. The name Salimbeni is carved into the wood lintel above one of the bedroom doors. Perhaps I'll scratch my name into a lintel somewhere, too.

I've given Alberto and Anna an honest and detailed explanation of the water situation, as far as I understand it. It doesn't bother them. They want to dig deeper into the well.

And there is an improvement. After my stay here two summers ago, my brother and I commissioned Fabbri and Generini to install larger cisterns at the side of the house, so that water can be collected over the winter. The same idea as Wenzel's, only that our cisterns are not quite as large. Both our cisterns and the Wenzels' have valves so that once they are full, the water will go to Renato's shed for his cows. He seems pleased enough with this arrangement.

It was a funny moment when I invited Renato up to Querceto to show him how our new system worked.

"But it's all broken in there," he said with a dismissive gesture as we approached the *stallina*. "Those wires, those machines lying on the ground."

"Oh, those," I said with an equally dismissive gesture as I unlocked the door. "Those are just old pumps. This new one works fine."

It only occurred to me later to wonder how, before I had even opened the door, he could have known it was "all broken in there." He must have managed to open the door on his own; it's a simple latch key, easy enough to duplicate. But he wasn't *furbo* enough to conceal his act from me. His desire to show off got the better of him.

Some things have changed, some remain the same.

Marino still plants beans and potatoes on our field below the bake house, and cuts the grass around Querceto twice a year.

Libby and Richard are doing well. The studio is finished. After all these years, I am at last allowed to enter it. It is a beautiful airy room, with French doors opening onto the terrace and a skylight in the high slanted ceiling. The parquet floor is a deep golden color, burnished with wax.

Stepping inside, I am surrounded by the fragrance of oil paints and turpentine.

On the left-hand wall are Libby's most recent paintings—small, intimate still-lifes. I am immediately attracted by one in particular and go up close to look at it. It shows four tangerines, a knife, and a pewter cup against a brown-black background. For some reason this picture moves me. Perhaps it's the way the objects lie separately on the table, not touching each other, and only the reflection in the cup seems to gather them together.

In the middle of the studio stands an easel with an unfinished canvas. Next to it, on a small table, are five rotting peaches in a bowl, some of them actually moldy.

Libby points to them with a laugh. "They always say still-lifes are about transience. It takes me so long to paint a flower bud that I can see it opening up in the process."

I feel envious. "How did you learn to do this? Did they teach you this at the academy?"

"No, I wasn't there long enough to work in oils. Signora Fini made you draw in charcoal for the first three years. I learned everything from watching Richard."

On the other side of the studio, Richard's canvases lean against the wall with their backs to the viewer.

"Can I see these?"

"No… They're mostly just old stuff, anyway."

Typical Richard.

"The studio is beautiful," I say, wanting to compliment him, too. "The walls are such a lovely color."

"It's just gray."

He is beginning to irritate me.

"No," I insist stubbornly, "it's not just gray. It has a soft bluish-green in it, like moss."

He then admits that he was trying to reproduce the precise color of the walls in Signora Fini's establishment, a particular hue that brought out the flesh tones of the models.

I feel stunned, like someone who has been tapping on a wall as a joke and suddenly hears a hollow sound. "What models?" I think. Whose flesh tones will be brought out? But maybe that isn't really the point. You think you know a person a little bit, and then you find out that they have been carrying a certain hard-to-describe color in their head for thirty years.

Richard has begun making signs to Libby, describing something with his hands while looking at her accusingly. He seems to be indicating an elongated object. Libby looks puzzled for a moment, then her face lights up.

"Oh, we have a strudel in the freezer, and Richard wants to know if we can have it."

"She won't make it just for us."

We sit on the terrace. It's almost like the old days.

"How's that dissertation coming along?" Richard teases me. "Still clattering away at the keyboard whenever someone passes by?"

"I finished it," I say. "I graduated. I seem to remember sending you an invitation. So, how about it? What about the two of you coming to visit me in America?"

He laughs and doesn't dignify that with a response.

He has no desire to leave the paradise he has created. It's his life's work. Even though the studio is finished, there is still more to do: an arch here, a balcony there. Libby, on the other hand, has bought a flat in London and she travels back and forth, alternating between city and countryside.

I ask about our Mugello neighbors.

"Ziegmann has mellowed a bit," Libby says. "He has a new girlfriend—she's English and she keeps him in line. Though there was a terrible hoo-ha a few months ago between him and Sabina about their dividing wall. Some branches hanging over it or something. They were at the point of coming to blows, and Renato had to go over and calm them down.

"But let's face it, Renato quite enjoys the excitement. I asked him once if he minded, and you know what he said? He said, 'In the old days, before the foreigners came, it used to be so quiet you'd hear nothing but birds and cicadas. Now at least there's something going on.'

"I think he was disappointed when he found out that you sold Querceto to an Italian family. He said the house is big enough you could have made four apartments out of it, and made millions renting them out to foreigners. He and Alessandra could have taken care of it. I think he envisions that as Lorenzo takes over more of the farm work, he might get a hand in the *agriturismo* business. The irony of it, you know, is that for all their hard work, now the Italian government is paying farmers *not* to cultivate their fields."

Lorenzo has married his girlfriend from Borgo and they have a baby. But his wife wants to continue working as a hairdresser. This is causing frictions in the family. The future of the farm is uncertain.

"And oh—we finally met your neighbor, Wenzel! He came by to ask about our hedges; he likes them better than the ones he's planted. He seems very nice, actually. He was bemoaning the fact that his five children want to go off on their own vacations and have no interest in coming here.

"And what about you, my dear? Are there any eligible bachelors on the horizon?"

32

The second time I visit Silvana she is waiting for me in her kitchen. She hugs me, but is dry-eyed this time. She repeats, "My life is finished."

I say that she and Costanzo were lucky to have had over fifty years together. "Not many couples are that lucky."

"Now it's all over," is her response. "When I take the pill the doctor prescribes for me, I don't cry anymore. But on days when I don't take it, I can't stop crying."

She suggests that we go see if there are "one or two cherries" on the tree in the garden. Sama comes with us.

"How Costanzo used to like to sit in this spot," she says when we come to the cherry tree, "where it's cool. Sometimes I still think I see him leaning on the fence in front of the house, in his usual place. He used to say, 'I feel comfortable here, leaning.'"

As we pick the cherries, she tells me that she lives in Vigliano now, but spends every other day at La Croce, where she still keeps her vegetable garden, her rabbits and her chickens.

"Costanzo's funeral was on a Saturday, on

Sunday we all came up here to put things in order, and already on Monday I came back by myself. Ever since then, I haven't stopped coming to La Croce, one day yes, one day no."

On alternate days she goes to the cemetery. On Sundays Enrico sometimes helps her with the larger chores. It isn't easy for her to get to and from La Croce. She takes the school bus as far as Riaccio and walks the rest of the way. The dogs know her, they don't bother her. I marvel that she can walk up that long, steep hill, at her age.

La Croce has become even quieter. Maia and Manfredo still spend several months each year in their converted school building. But Marietta and Salvatore have moved to Sardinia for good, and Elio has become house-bound, an invalid. I ask about Flavio. Silvana tells me that he is working for ANAS and also helping Renato in his spare time. When Costanzo was sick, very often it was Flavio who drove them to the hospital.

"Flavio is the man of La Croce now," she says, looking at me.

After we've picked a good bagful of cherries, Silvana tends to her chickens and I walk back to Querceto to get the car, so that I can give her a ride down to Vigliano. I wait while she changes her clothes in the back room. I can hear the soft sounds of garments being slipped on and off. She changes her stockings in the kitchen, replacing the thick ones with delicate ones for town. A new, elegant Silvana stands before me, in a dark skirt and pale green sweater, with a silk scarf knotted around her neck.

On Tuesday I go with Silvana to the cemetery to visit Costanzo's grave.

The cemetery is near the large shopping center in Borgo, surrounded by a high wall. As you enter the gate there is a small area for plots in the earth; but most of the tombs are in an open two-story structure above ground. Before going to Costanzo's tomb on the second floor, we visit the graves of his elder sister and Armanda's father. "Since you've brought so many flowers for Costanzo," Silvana says, "I might as well give mine to them, *poverini*."

From the moment we entered the cemetery gates, a kind of panic has taken hold of me. I breathe deeply to try to calm myself. All the gravestones have photographs on them. I look around, noticing the names, the faces in the photographs. There are a handful of other women visiting graves, not a single man. They bend over the photos and kiss them, with several quick little kisses like one gives a child.

The photo of Costanzo's sister bears a striking resemblance to Costanzo. I remark on this, and Silvana says, "Yes—she was so beautiful, and she loved him so much. If you could have seen her when she got married, with blond hair all the way down her back, big curls... She was still young when she died."

Costanzo could have had the spot next to her; they could have been side by side. But he had often expressed the wish not to be buried in the ground because the idea of all that rain soaking down into the earth bothered him. So they put him up on the second floor instead.

We go up the stairs. A marble wall bears four long rows of tombs. Costanzo's plaque is in the third row from the top. Two women stand nearby, and Silvana greets them in a low voice, deferentially; their greeting in return seems a little standoffish. They merely nod and keep standing there as if expecting something. Probably they have already finished arranging their flowers and there is nothing left for them to do. In front of Costanzo's grave Silvana hugs me fiercely, then whispers: "That woman has her husband *and* her son here. She's still young."

I feel as if the words, "still young, still young,"

were being muttered all around me.

Silvana wipes off Costanzo's photo with her hand—or perhaps caresses it—before leaning forward and kissing it. At first, she says, the photo bothered her, and she pleaded with Enrico to take it off. But now she is glad to have it there.

For a while, both of us are silent. Panic and the consciousness of having to express sadness make me unable to feel anything. I notice that the plaque next to Costanzo's belongs to a man whose name was Fortunato—an ironic name to appear on someone's tomb.

The color photo of Costanzo was taken at Alvise's communion. It's not a good picture. He looks uncomfortably stuffed into his suit and tie, the way little boys look who have been dressed by their mothers. His eyes and mouth are three slits around a rather malformed nose. I never noticed his nose while he was alive. His face has no expression at all.

I remember Costanzo as he was, the way he used to call out to me from the kitchen to come inside, his uneasiness when Silvana wasn't near, all his mannerisms and expressions and the sound of his voice. It's not difficult: he is perfectly present in my mind.

Finally I say, "Costanzo was a special person, a

very kind person." It seems that Silvana was only waiting for me to say this. "Yes: he was special. Good, and kind, and also *educato*, and *intelligente*."

I remember how he used to like to show his knowledge of the world, his facts and figures; I wonder if this was a sore point with him all his life.

"Costanzino, *poverino*. How he would like to be up at La Croce now, in the cool breeze, instead of walled-in here."

She begins to busy herself with the flowers I've brought, arranging them with care in the vase. I had stopped paying attention to the two women. Now, looking over, I see that one of them has climbed on a ladder and is polishing a plaque in the top row; the other has sprinkled sawdust on a spot of spilled water and is expertly moving it about with a broom before flicking it into the dustpan. It's all they can do not to start waxing the floors.

Silvana has some lilies left that can't be fit into her arrangement, and she offers them to the woman who has both her husband and son entombed here. I watch the interaction, Silvana so kindly and sweetly offering – "They're fresh, if you'd like them," the woman hesitant, not particularly friendly. Is there a class difference involved? Or is it my presence that is putting her off?

I tell Silvana I'm going for a walk, to give her some time by herself. She seems pleased. "Come back in half an hour, if you like." As she walks me as far as the stairs, another elderly woman approaches and they exchange murmured greetings. Silvana introduces me with an offhand gesture as "a friend of mine, *una tedesca*, she gave me a ride here by car."

"Ah, yes," her acquaintance says. "Otherwise I think you wouldn't be here yet at this time."

Unlike those other women, I sense that this is a friend, and they will have a little chat while I'm gone.

When I pick Silvana up from the cemetery, she seems to give herself a push and then says, "You know, don't you, that I have a place in Vigliano now?"

"No, I didn't know that." I'd assumed she was living with Enrico and Armanda.

"Let's go. I'll show it to you. We'll have a little snack there."

She directs me to park the car in front of one of the new buildings near the Co-op, around the corner from Enrico and Armanda's. I wonder if Enrico doesn't want her to tell me about the apartment.

The entrance hall is paved with marble. "Shall

we take the elevator or the stairs?" she asks, as if to point out that we have the luxury of a choice.

"My life is finished," she says as she unlocks the door.

We step into a handsome living room, high-ceilinged, the walls painted pale pink. Light streams in from a window giving onto a large balcony.

"It's *too* big for me," she laments. "What am I supposed to do with all this, by myself?"

She indicates the china cupboard. "I brought my good things down from La Croce. Otherwise, I'd be afraid of arriving up there one day and finding the place cleared out by Albanians." The gleaming modern bathroom is nearly as large as the kitchen at La Croce. "We sold some of our land. We sold some fields to Renato and to that Sicilian who lives up above Castellina."

Silvana is obviously proud of her new place and wants to hear it praised. Yet when I admire some aspect of it, she'll say, "It's all for nothing. I'm just living out my days in solitude, waiting to die." I make a sorrowful face, and she'll point out another detail that I haven't properly remarked on yet. "Do you like this nice big *terrazza*?"

But: "I never sit there. I only go out to clean it."

In the bedroom, some laces and embroidered

linen cloths are spread out on the double bed, her dowry or wedding presents, never used, as if she'd just been sorting through them. Perhaps she has laid them out for me to see? I realize that she intended all along to show me her apartment.

Among the photos on the dresser is a framed picture of her and Costanzo as newlyweds. Both of them look taller than in real life, as if the photographer had somehow contrived to stretch them out. Costanzo looks youthful and dapper in his suit, his light-colored hair two inches high on his head, the very image of a fine young man. Silvana is almost unrecognizable to me. Plump, with tight black curls, she has a severe, stalwart, battleship look about her that I can't reconcile with the tiny, gentle Silvana I know.

"Isn't it true," Silvana says, "he didn't change much, Costanzo. He never showed his age. Even at the end he looked like a young man, especially when he got dressed up. He enjoyed life so much."

I can't help remembering how, already two years ago, he had the aspect of someone who was tired of it all.

And again: "Do you like this apartment? Do you think it's nice?"

They had bought the apartment when he became ill, with the thought that he'd be better off down in Vigliano, close to the doctors and the hospital. "He could have sat out on the *terrazza,* watching the people come and go." The balcony overlooks the Co-op parking lot. "Or he could have walked over to the station bar; he loved to watch people playing those games. Everything is within easy reach. We wouldn't have had to be snowed in at La Croce. We could have had all this together, and instead—nothing."

It seems to me that Silvana is suffering because she can't help enjoying her luxurious new living quarters, even without Costanzo. "It's too much," she says, "too many things."

She offers me pear juice and cookies.

Before I leave, she gives me a little plastic-covered photo of Costanzo as a remembrance. Then she asks me once more if I like her apartment.

33

I am eating the last of the cherries Silvana gave me, that we picked the other day. Above the clouds, I hear the boom of a fighter plane flying at supersonic speed, on exercise from a military base somewhere nearby. It reminds me that there is a world outside this place.

And then again, before me on the terrace, a big snail has been making its way across the stones. In the space of several hours it has gone only about one meter.

This morning a very odd thing happened. I looked out one of the front windows toward La Croce and saw a male figure standing down by Elio's shed. It was no one I recognized. Instinctively I reached for my binoculars to get a better look. No sooner did I have the man in my view than I saw that he was looking back at me through a pair of binoculars bigger and stronger than mine. He must have raised them to his eyes at the same moment. We each simultaneously realized what the other was doing, and I saw him put his binoculars down half a second before I put mine down. Then he began walking quickly toward the left, where another man in an orange shirt had appeared.

He was probably going to tell his friend that he

had just seen *una tedesca* looking back at him through binoculars.

Silvana calls me in the early afternoon and asks what I'm doing. I am busy sorting through the contents of the wardrobes, packing things into bags and boxes which, little by little, I've been bringing down to the big trash dumpsters in Vigliano.

"*Niente.*"

"Do you feel like taking a walk with me in the woods?"

Having asked the question, she gets it into her head that she is disturbing me and begins to apologize, saying, "Never mind, if you're busy, it was just an idea."

I tell her that I need a break and can finish what I'm doing later.

"The tomatoes need work," she says. "I really ought to be putting stakes in them, but the garden is too wet after all that rain last night, and I can't bear the thought of staying pent up in the house all afternoon until Enrico comes to pick me up."

We meet halfway between Querceto and La Croce, where the path going up into the woods branches off. Silvana is carrying a walking stick and an umbrella, and has a canvas bag over the crook of her left arm; Sama is at her heels. "I'm happy to have your company," she says. "You like the woods too, don't you?" Not that she is afraid to go by herself, of course, she quickly adds.

"Perhaps we'll find a mushroom or two."

She takes the first steep stretch of the path steadily and easily, while I am huffing and puffing after a few minutes. We pass the formerly roofless house, which has been beautifully restored now. "Like a mansion," Silvana says, referring with a giggle to its owner as *Zucchino*. But she won't tell me the reason for this unflattering nickname.

"This is where Costanzo used to park the car when we came to look for mushrooms." I express surprise that a car can go up this road at all, steep and rocky as it is. "Oh yes," she says, "he used to drive up here or even further, sometimes into the woods as far as the cabin. He knew this road so well, maybe even better than the road to Vigliano. He often waited in the car for me while I went looking for mushrooms."

I can tell that she is happier as soon as we've entered the woods. "Vigliano is good for convenience," she says. "But this place is good *per la persona*."

It quickly becomes clear that her casual remark about finding "a mushroom or two" was the greatest understatement. We're not in the woods for five minutes, still far from reaching the cabin, when she suddenly climbs up an embankment and starts poking around in the leaves with the tip of her umbrella. Almost immediately – "Look at these *gallinelle!*" The word for chanterelles is "little hens." I didn't think she could be so happy about anything: she laughs with pure joy, encouraging me to pick the tiny yellow mushrooms as well. "There's another patch. You get those."

The first ones always come out under chestnut trees, she tells me. Only later do they come out under oak trees as well. "Who knows why?" But not just under any chestnut tree, only under certain ones. She speaks of mushrooms as "being born." "Who knows why they are born in one spot and not another?"

I find a patch of *gallinelle* that Silvana has missed. She is delighted, and seems surprised that she didn't see them first, since she knows all the exact spots. The patch I've found is even larger than the others, five or six mushrooms instead of three or four. "You see, after last night's rain..."

Then there are no more, and we return to the path. "Perhaps we'll find one or two more later on."

I feel that her happiness of a moment earlier is gone.

We must look like an odd pair. Silvana, at my side, is so much smaller than me that it gives me a feeling of wanting to protect her.

When the path gets narrower and steeper, she walks ahead of me. Every once in a while, she speaks a few words of encouragement. "Go slowly. Be careful. *Niente furia*. Come along. *Attenta*. Watch out."

The ground is covered in yellowish and light brown leaves. There are bad chestnuts that were left lying last year, and empty, prickly hulls.

I become fixated on finding more *gallinelle* for Silvana. Her spirits seem to have dropped again, and I can tell she is searching one after the other all the spots where they usually grow. I can't help hoping that I might be able to surprise her again. My eyes are focused intently on the ground; I keep mistaking some small yellowish leaf for a mushroom, only to be disappointed.

We walk by the cabin, but she avoids going near it, much less entering inside—even though before, when it looked as though we were going to be finding loads of mushrooms, she mentioned having another plastic bag in the cabin.

"How much Costanzo slept in there!" she remarks as we pass it.

"He slept?"

Yes, she'd fixed up a proper bed inside, and he would nap while she and Enrico went about the work of clearing the undergrowth and gathering the chestnuts.

"In the last years he worked very little. I was keeping it going by myself, with Enrico."

"Maybe he was tired."

"*Macché* tired! He could rest!" There is anger in her voice.

"If only I could have him back just for company," she says, her tone changing again to sadness. "I'd gladly take care of the work, if only he could sit there and keep me company. Elio, even though he does nothing but sit in his chair, at least he's there, for company, to eat with."

I wonder if this is an ongoing discussion between her and Paola. Who is worse off, Paola with her husband who is alive, but might as well be dead, or Silvana with her husband who is dead, but of whom at least she has good memories? "Elio at least is *there*," Silvana says. "Costanzo's gone."

She says, "*Costanzo non c'è più*," several times

during the course of our walk, in brief, staccato syllables that express a sense of finality and, it seems to me, the absence of any religious consolation.

As we walk on, Silvana goes back and forth between talking about mushrooms and talking about Costanzo. The two subjects merge seamlessly. The same lament refers sometimes to Costanzo and sometimes to the absence of mushrooms. "Here, you can see there are few mushrooms—*macché* few, there are none, *punti, punti!* Not even a *pinarolo*, not even one! Nothing! *Nulla, nulla!*" We poke around in the leaves. "How hard he worked all his life, Costanzo! How he labored! He got a good pension when he retired; he could have enjoyed life, in our apartment down in Vigliano. He wouldn't have had to do anything, I would have done it all. But instead—*nulla!*"

We clamber up and down paths that aren't paths at all. I have no idea where we are. If I were by myself, I would be hopelessly lost.

"See, someone else has been here before us," Silvana says suddenly, pointing at the ground. I can't see anything. It seems highly unlikely to me that someone else would have been traipsing around this remote part of the woods this very morning, knowing all the same spots that Silvana knows and snatching the little *gallinelle* away.

After a while she says, "Perhaps it's because these places are a little higher than where we found the first ones, that there are none. You see, the air is a little cooler up here, and perhaps these spots are getting less sun. There must be some difference, if there were mushrooms down there and not here."

At one point she asks me, "Right, you wouldn't be able to find these paths on your own?" Behind this question I imagine Enrico's concern about family secrets being given out.

Suddenly there is a gap in the trees, and I see a house on the slope opposite, a little lower than where we are standing. It's La Roccia; I didn't recognize it at first from this angle. I am surprised that we've climbed so quickly to a point higher than La Roccia. We are much higher than Castellina, which I now spot to the left.

"Yes, that's La Roccia. The woman goes to work, somewhere near Borgo, I think. Who knows what it is she does there."

I remember with shame my anecdote about Brigitte Mandelbaum and remain silent.

"The husband just stays up at the house all the time."

"But he is much older than she is," I say, to excuse him.

"Yes, he's old. And sometimes he makes certain old-man cries..."

I let this sink in for a moment. "What do you mean, he makes cries? Do you mean he sings?"

"No, he makes cries, like this—*Aaah aah!* Like a *capriolo*. We were frightened the first time we heard it. He is very strange."

I feel it necessary to stand up for Gustav Mandelbaum. I tell Silvana that he used to be a very important professor in Berlin, and he lost everything because he was Jewish.

Silvana makes a suitably grave sound and then remarks that in his cellar, which was open once when she and Enrico passed by, there was a strange sort of rug with saints lined up on it. "That must be where he goes to pray." She looks at me questioningly.

"Were they Christian saints?" Perhaps he has an art collection.

"No, no, they were different. They must belong to that religion you just mentioned."

We walk on in silence.

All the other places that Silvana knows, one after the other, are empty. The woods are pierced by her cries: Not even one! Not even a shadow of a *gallinella*! Not even a *pinarolo*! *Nulla, nulla!* I'm sure that the Parkers, down at Castellina, can hear her.

We come to a clearing, and Silvana suggests that we sit down to rest on a fallen tree trunk. Sama scampers around us, but with less energy than usual. It turns out that Silvana has a little surprise for me. She was carrying a picnic in the canvas bag. Tea with sugar and lemon, filled into a plastic water bottle, and delicious apple fritters that she made before we set out. "Do you like them? Eat them, eat them all. I ate too many before, while I was making them. Do you like them? Costanzo used to love these. But even more, he loved fried rice balls."

"That Friday," she says, after we've eaten for a few minutes in silence, listening to the sounds of the woods, "I was alone with him in the hospital. He'd been bad all day, breathing with difficulty, moving about in bed, agitated. It was about 7:30, he was turning back and forth, and I said to him, 'Calm down, or you'll get out of breath.' And he said, 'I already am.' He rolled over on his side, away from me, and I thought he had calmed down, but he was dead. Just like that. *In un nulla!*"

In a nothing! she repeats several times more, after telling me this story.

"What time is it?" We've been resting for a while. "But who cares what time it is, since Costanzo isn't at home waiting for me. Anyway, at least we've had a good walk, right?"

Despite such statements of resignation, Silvana's hope of finding more mushrooms seems to have revived. "We can take a different way down. I know one or two other spots, if you're not too tired."

We set out again, single file, following a tiny trail made by *caprioli*. From time to time Silvana stops and looks more intently, poking in the leaves with the tip of her umbrella.

"They are only born in certain precise spots, not even areas or zones but under this or that specific tree. Sometimes it's an old chestnut tree, sometimes a young one. Who knows why they are born in one spot and not another?"

She picks up a walking stick for me, worried that I might have trouble following her on the difficult terrain. "Be careful. Go slowly. There's no rush." I have no trouble walking, but the stick helps me focus my eyes. I feel that everything depends on our finding more of those mushrooms. I am so intent on looking at the ground that at times I scarcely even pay attention to what she is saying or to our surroundings. It reminds me of my dream of going with Generini, following the course of the water tube.

"Now we're in Flavio's woods," Silvana remarks suddenly, and a little later, "now we're in Elio's woods." I ask her how she can tell where the boundary is. She is nonplussed by my question. "You see that tree over there? That belongs to Flavio, and these over here are all Elio's."

Whereas Flavio's *marroneta* is well-kept, with the brush cleared and neatly cut tree boughs stacked up here and there, Elio's is woefully neglected.

"Look at this, all ruined."

Whole fallen trees are blocking our way. As we pass a large chestnut tree, I see a wine flask hidden under one of its roots. I point it out to Silvana, but she doesn't seem surprised. "That's Elio's," she says dismissively. "He used to bring along something to drink when he came up into the woods."

We come to a clearing where the sun shines through the trees. And here suddenly – "Look at all the little poisonous ones! They're a good sign," she says, "*poverini.*"

A minute later, sure enough, there is a spot of *gallinelle.* "Look, look!"

It's an even bigger patch than our first one.

Silvana is happy again. "There are some more

over there, *you* take those." She gives me the empty box from the fritters to put them in.

"Look at these, poor things: they're still tiny. They were born only a little while ago. They were born just this minute."

"The woods gives everything." We are walking downhill again. I am surprised how quickly we are back in familiar territory. It seems we've been roaming endlessly, and then in no time we are back by the cabin again.

"The woods gives us everything," Silvana resumes after we've passed the cabin in silence. "Chestnuts, mushrooms. It does it all by itself."

"Water," I add, seeing the bundle of tubes from La Croce's springs once again by the side of the path.

"Water," she agrees.

I remember all my adventures of two years ago. Alberto and Anna will pick up where my family left off. They will dig their well or wells and get to know a diviner or two. They will get to know Renato and Lorenzo, and others. I suspect that the problem of water at Querceto will never be completely resolved. It will just keep on shifting and changing, like life itself.

And with one thing and another, the years will go by for them too: happily, I hope.

34

After my outing into the woods with Silvana, I see no one for several days. I am busy with countless errands and preparations for handing over the house. Although I've made myself lists and planned as best I could, there is much more to do at the end than I anticipated.

Four days after our walk, Silvana calls me in the early afternoon. She tells me that Paola was in the woods yesterday and didn't find any mushrooms, so probably there won't be any today either. It's only as she tells me this that I remember we had discussed the possibility of going a second time. It had completely slipped my mind. She is calling now to say, "Let's not go;" but I feel ashamed because, in my busyness, I forgot about her.

"My head chose this path," she says, the last time I visit her at La Croce. She is leaning on the kitchen table much as Costanzo used to, speaking of her decision immediately after his death to go to La Croce one day and to the cemetery the next, in strict alternation, "one day yes, one day no." She has not deviated from this routine except during a brief period when she was ill. "Who knows if it's right or wrong, or good or bad. It's to make the time pass by."

I try bringing up other topics, my trip, the people who will take over Querceto soon. But she wants to talk about herself. It's as if, leaning on the kitchen table, she wants to provide a sort of summing-up, to say to me: "This is my life."

She tells me that the other day when she went to the cemetery, no one else was there and she was so tired that she fell asleep sitting on a chair. "I was so fast asleep that when I woke up I thought I was at home in bed, until I saw the wreaths. It's a good thing I didn't fall off the chair, I could have hurt myself on that marble floor! From now on, whenever I go, I'll have a coffee beforehand."

I have come to say goodbye. I decline her offer of something to drink and only sit down for a few minutes.

I walk down to Renato's farm to say goodbye to him and Alessandra. Lorenzo and his wife are there and I admire their plump baby, who looks just like the photo of Lorenzo that used to be on the kitchen wall.

On my last evening I have dinner with Libby and Richard. "We know you'll be back," they assure me, and reiterate their offer of the guest room.

Afterward, they both drive me back to Querceto. We shake hands ceremoniously, with exaggerated formality.

On the day of departure, I am ready to go by noon. The house is clean and empty except for the furniture; my luggage and the last bags of garbage are packed into the back of the Uno. I say goodbye to Marino, who is working in his field.

A few minutes later, there is a knock at the door. I run to open it and find myself facing two men dressed in suits and ties. My first thought is that I've run afoul of the law somehow. My mind races to the car registration that expired more than a decade ago and the mountains of trash I've been depositing in the dumpsters in Vigliano. Then one of the men opens a briefcase stuffed with magazines, and I realize they are Jehova's Witnesses.

"I'm sorry, but I don't have time right now," I say. "I'm about to leave for America."

"In that case, perhaps you'd like something to read on the way?" The man with the briefcase adds, "You've probably guessed who we are."

The second man has extraordinary, light-colored, half-moon-shaped eyes in which the irises can't be distinguished. Distracted by these uncanny eyes looking at me, I accept a magazine. At that moment there is a loud rustling in the grass by the side of the house. The half-moon eyes look alarmed.

"A snake," I say nonchalantly.

"Aren't you afraid?"

"Not as long as it's moving away from me," I say, smiling at the silliness of my reply.

We shake hands. They wish me a good flight, and I wish them—I see no car—a good walk.

I check all the doors and shutters once more to make sure everything is tightly locked, even though it doesn't really matter since the new owners will be coming shortly. I start the engine and drive slowly up the slope, the Uno laboring under the unaccustomed weight. Branches of Scotch broom loaded with yellow blossoms brush against the car from the side of the path.

As I approach La Croce I see Silvana at work in her garden. I drive slowly, thinking I might stop one last time. She comes up to where the hedge shields the garden from the path and peers through the branches at me, not realizing that I've already seen her. Her face has that blank expression with which you can sometimes catch people looking at you when they think themselves unobserved.

I decide not to stop. As I drive on to the train station I remember the last thing she said to me. *Grazie per la compagnia.* Thank you for your company.

I think that is perhaps the best we can ever say to each other. It hardly makes a difference whether people are married for a lifetime or friends for one hour.

ACKNOWLEDGEMENTS

First and foremost, I wish to thank Julian Anderson, my brilliant editor, for "leading the horse to water" and helping to bring this work to completion. I am deeply grateful to her and to Jennifer Harris and Mary Bisbee-Beek at JackLeg Press for their faith and enthusiasm.

My special thanks to Caroline Walker Bynum and Victoria Hutchinson, for their extraordinary friendship and support.

I dedicate this book to William Caferro, my "co-conspirator," who first drew my attention to the epigraph on the clock, and to many other things.

ABOUT THE AUTHOR

Megan Weiler was born in Philadelphia and grew up in Konstanz, Germany. She was educated at the Heinrich Suso Gymnasium, Bryn Mawr College, and Yale. Her first novel, *The Night Bell*, was published in 2001 by Picador UK. Early short stories appeared in *Mississippi Review* and *Nimrod*; her story "Wolfenbüttel" was published 2021 in *Common Knowledge*, along with an excerpt from her unpublished novel *A World Without Echoes*. She lives with her husband in Nashville.

JACKLEG PRESS

CPSIA information can be obtained
at www.ICGtesting.com
Printed in the USA
BVHW031743070222
628313BV00001B/36